*Realms Of The Fae 1
A Debt Owed*

Realms Of The Fae 1
A Debt Owed

Avril Sabine

Cracked Acorn Productions
Australia

Realms Of The Fae 1: A Debt Owed

Published by

Cracked Acorn Productions

PO Box 1365

Gympie, Queensland 4570

Australia

978-1-925131-48-2 (Kindle)

978-1-925131-49-9 (EPUB)

978-1-925131-49-9 (Print)

Genre: Young Adult Urban Fantasy

Cover design by Caitlyn Petersen

For my children, who spent a lot of time helping me look for fairies, elves and trolls when they were younger. Hope you had as much fun as I did.

Melody's mum made a bargain with the Fae twenty years ago, but she's the one who ends up paying for it. Somehow she has to survive nearly a year in the realms of the Fae, until her eighteenth birthday, without getting more entangled in their world and unable to ever leave it. The Fae can be vindictive, manipulative and retaliate at the smallest slight, often using your greatest fears against you. Melody needs to make sure they never learn how terrified she is of spiders, particularly when helping a Fae knight brings her to the attention of his enemies, the arachnid people.

*

This story was written by an Australian author using Australian spelling.

Name Pronunciation

Like many names there is more than one way to pronounce the following ones. These are the pronunciations used in this story.

Aderyn (ad-ur-en)

Brynn (brin)

Carden (car-den)

Dione (dee-own)

Elon (ee-lon)

Eolande (yoh-lahn-duh)

Fileas (fill-ee-as)

Pirro (peer-o)

Rhodri (rod-dree)

Seren (sair-wren)

Chapter One

Melody Atwood stubbed her toe on the kitchen bench, reaching for the tap to fill the glass she'd taken from the draining rack. There was no way she was going to turn the light on. It'd only wake her up and it had been hard enough to fall asleep in this heat, without making it any more difficult to return to sleep. It had been the worst time of all for the air conditioner to die. Brisbane in January without an air con wasn't fun. At least tomorrow she'd be going to her dad's place for the week. Hopefully the air con would be fixed before she came back to her mum's in time to start year twelve. It didn't seem possible that this was her last year of high school.

Finished her drink, she sat the glass beside the sink and lifted her damp hair from the back of her neck, yawning. The house hadn't been designed to survive summers without air-conditioning. With another yawn, she let go of her hair and headed towards the hallway.

Reaching it, Melody squinted her eyes against the soft glow of the nightlight that had been in the hallway for as long as she could remember. She wiped her damp hands against the oversized cotton t-shirt she wore to bed, reaching for the wall again as she stumbled in her half awake state. A couple more steps and she reached her bedroom. She froze, all traces of sleep vanishing.

A backwards step made her feel no better. Her heart raced, her eyes wide as she stared at the huntsman spider on her floor. Its eight hairy legs appeared ten times their actual size and she opened her mouth to call for her mum. Only a squeak escaped. She backed up more, hitting the hallway wall behind her. Inching along the hallway, the wall against her back, Melody was unable to take her gaze from the spider. It was nearly as big as a side plate.

She sent a glance towards the closed door of her mum's study at the end of the hall, light shining under the gap. Her gaze was drawn back to the spider who still hadn't moved. Did she have time to get her mum and return before the spider scuttled away? She'd never sleep if it disappeared somewhere in her room. But she couldn't spend the entire night pressed up against the wall in the hallway. Her dad wouldn't be impressed if she wasn't ready when he arrived to pick her up at eight.

She blinked, hating the need that forced her to take her gaze off the creature for even a second. How was she going to cross the entire hallway to her mum's study if she couldn't even stand to take her gaze off the spider long enough to blink?

It was the city for crying out loud. The middle of Brisbane. You'd think spiders would be smaller here. Huntsman spiders belonged in the country. Not in the middle of the city.

Melody sighed. Who was she kidding? She'd still be frozen against the wall even if it was a daddy long legs spider. The huntsman chose that moment to scuttle towards her and, with a shriek, Melody dashed along the hall. She flung open the study door and slammed it shut behind her. Breathing hard, she tried to find the power of speech. She gestured to the closed door as her mum turned in her office chair to face her, the glow of the computer screen and a desk lamp the only light in the dimly lit room.

"Mum, there's a-" Speech deserted her again when her gaze was drawn by movement from across the room.

A man rose to his feet from the armchair that was

pushed between two towering and cluttered bookcases. He was several inches over six foot and almost painfully thin, his body all wiry muscle. He stalked towards Melody, his gaze raking over her, a vivid blue in his extremely pale skin, his long hair fair enough to be almost white. A slim hand reached out and tilted her head back with a gentle pressure on her chin. He smiled. "Where have you been keeping this delightful creature?"

The expression on his face caused Melody to take a hasty step backwards. The timber door prevented further retreat. If it wasn't for the spider, she would have opened the door and left her mum to her unsettling visitor. He seemed strangely dressed, almost old fashioned with his tall leather boots, fitted trousers, brocade vest and a leather pouch on his belt.

The man twined a lock of her long hair around his fingers. "Lovely. Not as fair as your mother's hair, but this golden colour has a beauty all of its own." When Melody dragged the strands from him he smiled, capturing her chin between his fingers. "Not as fine a face as those of our race, but your eyes remind me of a forest. A blend of shadowy greens. You'd make a lovely addition to the court."

Again Melody pulled from his grip. Who did he think he was?

Sherry rose to her feet, walking towards her daughter. "Excuse me a moment and then we can return to our business." She reached for the door handle.

"I believe we have other business to deal with now."

Melody wished the man would stop looking at her. It was making her extremely uncomfortable. Like she was some sort of exhibition in a freak show.

Sherry let her arm fall back to her side as she slowly turned to face the man. "What business?"

"A debt owed."

Sherry shook her head. "You can't be serious. I was too young to understand exactly what I was agreeing to. And grieving. My mother had just died."

Melody struggled to figure out what was going on. Her mum had known this man twenty years ago? Her grandmother had died three years before she'd been born. Why had she never met him? He would have been a toddler twenty years ago. Or a young child. What sort of deal would her mum have made with a kid?

"You're obligated to give me what I ask for."

Sherry continued to shake her head. "No, Elon. Please. Don't do this to me. Ask for something else."

Elon laughed. "You said anything. Haven't I kept

my end of the bargain? Aren't you famous? Don't your tales of the Fae sell to millions? Didn't I help prevent you from being a one hit wonder?"

"Please. You can't have her."

"Mum?" Melody looked uncertainly between the two, wondering if it wouldn't be better to face the huntsman after all. "What's going on?" Surely Elon couldn't have had anything to do with her mum's books. At the most he was in his mid twenties.

Sherry continued to stare at Elon. "Go to your room, Melody."

Elon shook his head. "Do you really want to do that? I can destroy what I've given you and still end up with her. Don't fight me on this and no harm will come to her from me."

"Mum?" This time the word was a whisper. Surely her mum wouldn't make her go with Elon. This was crazy.

"Will you protect her from all others?"

Melody stared at the back of her mum. Had she heard right? She stepped to the side so she could see her mum's expression. It didn't help. She had no idea what her mum was thinking.

"You have nothing else to bargain with."

"I'll give you anything. Whatever you want, it's yours."

Elon chuckled. "Didn't we have this exact conversation twenty years ago? Although you sound more desperate now than you did back then. The toast of the literary world, at nineteen, with your bestseller. Yet not even the glimmer of a story three years later when I met you. You made your bargain back then, now you must abide by it."

Melody didn't want to hear another word. She reached for the door handle and tried to open it enough to slip through. Her mum was in the way. Even when she pressed the door against her mum's back, she didn't move.

"Don't even think about it."

The tone in Elon's voice had Melody looking over her shoulder at him. A shiver went through her at his piercing gaze. She wanted to argue with him, but fear had her remaining silent. Her mum couldn't let her go with Elon. Her mum hadn't let her attend a party this week because there hadn't been adult supervision. She'd turned seventeen at the start of last month and didn't need a babysitter. Especially not at a party.

Sherry put an arm around Melody and drew her close. "She's not a piece of property to give away at will."

"She's a child and as such belongs to you according

to our laws. Don't fight me on this, Sherry. You won't like what happens."

"Do you think I'll like this any better?" Sherry's arm tightened around Melody.

At any other time, Melody would have pulled away. At five foot six she was as tall as her mum, but right this moment she wished she was short enough to hide behind her.

"Let go of the child and give her to me. You're starting to bore me and I did tell you if that was to ever happen there'd be no more stories. Including not finishing the one we've been working on tonight."

"Give me the terms. There must be some way she can end this bargain. In less than a year she'll be considered an adult. Does that mean she can leave once she turns eighteen?"

Elon laughed. "Do you honestly believe she could last nearly an entire year in my world without becoming indebted to someone else? She is human."

The way he spoke the word human had Melody wanting to ask him that if he thought so little of humans, why would he want her to go with him? None of this made sense. For the smallest moment she wondered if she was having a nightmare, but her dreams were never this real. And her nightmares never contained spiders the size of the one that had been in her room. They were always as large as her.

"If she makes it to her eighteenth birthday, when I celebrate it in this world, she's free of all obligations to you," Sherry said.

"This could be entertaining." Elon nodded thoughtfully. "I won't return her though. She'll have to find her own way back. Nor will I offer her any advice or protect her from others."

"But you won't harm her."

"I've already agreed to that. Do we have a bargain?"

"Yes. Give me half an hour to pack her things and say goodbye."

The scent of old rainforests filled the room, going as quickly as it came. "You can have half that time." Elon looked from one to the other. "Do not keep me waiting." He strode back to the armchair and dropped in it.

Melody stared at him. Her mum was going to make her leave with a stranger? Before she could protest, Sherry was drawing her from the room, closing the door behind them.

"We don't have much time," Sherry whispered.

Melody started to argue, stopping when she saw the spider in the hallway across from her door. She pointed towards it. "Mum, I can't-"

Sherry clamped a hand over her mouth. "Don't say it. Whatever you do, never let them know." She dragged Melody towards her room, pushing her through the doorway.

Melody stumbled as she tried to keep an eye on the spider and at the same time pull away from her mum. "What's going on?"

"They're all true. Every single book I've ever written, other than the first."

"But they're stories. About made up people." Melody eyed her mum. "Are you okay? Should I ring someone for you?"

"We don't have much time. You have to go with Elon. We don't have a choice. He'd take you anyway, but this way you have a chance of eventually returning home." As she spoke, Sherry grabbed a medium sized cloth backpack and started shoving clothes in it. "You have to remember everything I've ever written about the Fae. Your life could depend on it."

"I'm not going with him." There was no way her mum could make her. Besides, she could always move in with her dad.

Sherry shoved the backpack at Melody. She slipped off the gold charm bracelet she wore and held it out. "They love gold so each one of these charms will be valuable to them. Don't put yourself in anyone's debt. Go on, take it."

Chapter Two

Melody stared at the twenty-two charms attached to the links of the bracelet. Her mum never took it off. The charms had been a gift from her own mother, every birthday until she'd died. Everything all became frighteningly real. "There's an Elon in your books."

Sherry nodded.

"You can't make me go with him. If everything in your books is real, you can't make me go with him. I won't survive." Her voice broke on the last word.

Sherry slipped the bracelet over Melody's wrist and wrapped her arms around her. "I'm sorry. I was young and desperate. Don't you do anything so stupid. I didn't know what they were like, but you do. You've read all my books. Several times."

"I can't go." She'd rather face a room full of spiders. Well, maybe not quite that many.

"Get dressed. Quickly. We need to pack some food

for you to take. I'll meet you in the kitchen." Sherry let her go and strode across the room to fling the door open before striding down the hallway.

Melody grabbed jeans and a t-shirt, pulling them on before slipping her feet into a pair of sneakers. She crept towards her doorway, looking for the spider. It was gone. She ran after her mum, not wanting to be left alone in an area where a spider was hiding. "Did you hear me before? I can't go."

Sherry had turned on the kitchen light and was rummaging in the pantry. "Bring your backpack over here."

"Mum." She moved to stand beside her mum and watched as food was jammed inside the bag. Crackers, trail mix, chocolate bars, a packet of sweet biscuits, muesli bars, dried fruit, three tins of spaghetti and two one-litre bottles of water. The bag looked lumpy and strained at the seams.

"I'm sorry I don't have more to give you. I know it won't last long, but whatever you do, don't eat their food without taking the right precautions."

"Are you listening to me, Mum? I can't go with him."

"You don't have a choice. We don't have a choice. This way you have a chance of surviving and getting away. Fight him on it and he might never let you go. The Fae like a challenge." She reached out to rest a hand against Melody's cheek. "I didn't want this part of my life to ever touch yours. I did everything possible to keep you from meeting Elon. You should have been asleep. It's well after midnight and you've got an early morning. I'd thought it was safe to call him so we could continue to work on our latest story."

"It was too hot. I got up for a drink. And then there was a spider-"

Sherry covered her mouth again, glancing over her shoulder. "No, don't even speak of them. Never, ever show the Fae any fear. They'll use it against you. Never give them an advantage."

She drew away from her mum, alternating between accepting it was real and not believing a single word. "What about dad? What are you going to tell him?"

"I have no idea. He'll probably call the police." Sherry took her hand. "Come on. Before Elon comes looking for us."

She wanted to argue, but let her mum lead her back to the study, her mind full of the stories she'd grown up on. If even half of them were real, she didn't stand a chance. She even forgot the spider that had disappeared until they stepped into the study. A glance around showed it wasn't in here. At least not anywhere she could see.

Elon rose to his feet. "Are you ready now?"

"Yes," Sherry said.

At the same time, Melody shook her head.

"Didn't your mother explain? You have no choice in this," Elon said. "The bargain has been made."

"No, I mean yes, she did explain, but that's not what this is about." Still clutching the bulging backpack, she strode to the desk. "I have to leave my dad a note. Well, actually both my parents."

"Why would you need to leave your mother a note when she's standing right here?" Elon asked.

Melody didn't bother to explain. Instead she wrote a note to her parents telling them that going to year twelve was a waste of time when she didn't even know what she wanted to do with her life, other than travel. She didn't need to finish school to do that. She'd be in touch down the track. Behind her she heard her mum start to cry and she rose to her feet to wrap an arm around her. "I couldn't let him blame you or call the police."

"You believe me?"

How could she not? Her mum had given her the only possession she still had from her childhood. She drew back, staring at her mum's tearstained face.

"Yes." The only other time she'd seen her mum cry was when she'd spoken of returning home twenty years ago to find smoke and flames billowing from her family home, as firemen tried to put it out. She hadn't realised straight away that her mother had died in the fire, not until one of the neighbours had broken the news to her. "I'll see you on the seventh of December."

"Their time doesn't run the same as ours."

"I know."

Elon stepped forward and grabbed Melody's arm. "This is all very touching, but also extremely tedious." He looked towards Sherry. "Don't bother calling me to finish the story until after this bargain has ended." He turned to Melody. "Time to go." He drew a crumpled leaf from his pocket and tossed it on the ground. Still holding onto her arm, he stepped forward onto the leaf, drawing her with him.

The world shimmered around her, reforming to become a forest clearing, a white horse tethered nearby. It was early morning and as much as Melody wanted to draw away from Elon, she was worried he might leave her here in the middle of nowhere. Other than trees, shrubs and the horse, there was nothing else in sight.

Elon strode towards the horse, pulling her with him. "Can you ride?"

She shook her head.

Elon smiled. "This is going to be fascinating. I give you a week before you're so caught in my world you'll never have a chance to return to your own."

"What has riding got to do with anything?"

"That's the main form of transport here."

She wanted to disagree with him. Not being able to ride wouldn't stop her from surviving. She'd walk if necessary. Instead of arguing, she thought of her mum's stories. She had to be smart if she wanted to return home. "What do you bet that I'll last more than a week?"

"You have nothing to bet in return."

She raised her arm so the charms dangled from the bracelet. "One of these. What do you offer in return?"

Elon's gaze remained on her arm for a moment before he met hers. "What did you want?"

"Riding lessons. I want to learn how to ride."

He laughed, throwing his head back. When he eventually stopped, he stared at her, a smile remaining. "Seven days of my time."

She nodded, taking the hand he offered her, smelling the scent of old rainforests again. She could do this. There was no way that she wanted to spend the rest of her life here. The Fae didn't think very much of humans. Remembering her first thought had been that she wouldn't survive, the second that she didn't stand a chance, she pushed those thoughts from her. Somehow she had to figure it out so she did. If Elon thought it was important for her to be able to ride, then she needed to learn. When he let go of her hand and stared at her, she remained silent, worried she'd say something that would get her caught up in this world and unable to leave it.

Eventually Elon turned away and gathered the reins of the horse, swinging into the saddle. He held out a hand to her and when she took it, seated her behind him. Still clutching her backpack, she held onto Elon as he rode through the forest.

She hoped he knew where he was going because everything looked the same to her. When they came out of the forest to see open meadows leading towards a castle, set in landscaped gardens, she guessed he must have known the way. As much as she wanted to ask him more about the castle, she didn't dare say a word. Her mum's stories were full of humans, and even Fae, tricked into making promises they'd rather not keep. When Elon helped her dismount at the front of the castle, she fleetingly wondered if her mum would write this into a story.

She guessed that would only be possible if she escaped.

Elon handed the reins of his horse to a human, who came forward with gaze lowered. "Put him in the stable." He barely spared Melody a glance. "Don't get lost." He strode towards the open castle doors and inside.

Melody struggled to keep up. The last thing she wanted to do was get lost. The only person she could trust not to harm her was Elon, but there was no one she could trust to protect her. Somehow she'd have to manage that on her own. It was a struggle to keep up with Elon's long stride. She barely had time to take notice of her surroundings.

They passed other tall, slim, pale skinned people, some with their hair drawn back from their faces so she could see the slight point to the tips of their ears. There were humans amongst them. Mostly servants, some dressed up and treated like ornaments, one even on a leash held by an elaborately dressed woman. They travelled down corridors, twisting and turning through the building until they stepped into a crowded room.

Melody heard snippets of conversations as they made their way through the well-dressed crowd. "What can you expect? His mother was dark Fae."

A man nodded knowingly. They moved on before Melody could find out who they were speaking about. The next full sentence she heard was, "He won't last much longer. It's been three days already." A man replied, "He should have known better than to mess with the arachnid people."

The word arachnid made her shudder and she looked over her shoulder at the two men who were speaking, wondering if they spoke of the same person as the last couple. When she looked forward again, it was in time to reach the front of the crowd. She came to a stumbling stop, her gaze drawn to the woman talking to the crowned man sitting on a throne, an empty one to the right of him. The woman reminded her of a centaur. Where a centaur had the lower half of a horse, the woman was part arachnid. Her eight hairy legs were topped by the upper body of a woman with dusky coloured skin, thick black hair piled atop her head, and a bodice that looked like it was made from spider's web.

If the sight of the woman hadn't frozen her to the spot, Melody would have run from the throne room. As it was, she couldn't take her gaze from the woman and it took several minutes for the angry words she yelled at the king, to make sense.

"Enough, Dione." The king rose to his feet.

Melody struggled to think of his name. Why hadn't her mum written about the spider woman? If she had, there was no way she'd have entered the castle.

"I want him. He killed one of mine. I deserve to have him." Dione pointed to the left of the throne.

Melody glanced in that direction, then looked again. A young man stood in the corner, unable to leave it because of the chain on his leg. He looked to be shorter than Elon, about six foot, and had long dark hair and a more muscular build. He was still fairly slim, but not to the point that Elon and the rest of the fair haired Fae were. His arms were crossed over his bare chest and he wore only fitted trousers, his feet also bare. His expression was neutral, but he couldn't keep the anger from his brown eyes. A sheathed sword lay on the floor out of his reach.

"Brynn tells a different story," the king said.

"He lies," Dione snarled.

The king walked closer to Brynn, stopping near the sword. "Do you lie? Did you kill Dione's man for sport?"

"He attacked a human in the forest," Brynn said.

"The human came onto my lands." Dione pointed at Brynn. "You lie. You killed my knight for sport."

She turned to the king. "I demand him for my own. His life in payment for the one he stole."

A tall woman joined them. A jewelled crown nestled in her long fair hair that was piled upon her head to show her pointed ears. She took a sip from the goblet she held and smiled at Dione. "You aren't still harping over this matter, are you? He's being punished for taking up arms against your knight. Surely you can lay the matter to rest now."

Seeing the two rulers together, Melody remembered their names. Queen Eolande and King Rhodri. But she'd never heard of Brynn. How many others hadn't her mum written about? Was that her choice or had it been because Elon hadn't mentioned them? She'd thought she'd have an advantage from all she'd read. She was beginning to think she didn't. That there was far too much she didn't know about the Fae.

"Wouldn't you avenge the death of one of your knights?" Dione demanded.

Eolande moved closer to Brynn. "Do you feel punished?"

"I've done nothing wrong, Your Majesty," Brynn said.

"Are you trying to tell me you're happy with being left chained without food or drink?" Eolande moved even closer, stopping so that the toes of her shoes almost touched the sword.

"No, Your Majesty."

"Are you saying you would like a drink?" She held out her goblet. "Are you thirsty, Brynn?"

He didn't speak, only held Eolande's gaze.

She laughed. "Maybe you'll stay out of what doesn't concern you in the future." She placed her goblet on the floor, near the sword. "Humans aren't worth your trouble." She turned away from him and stepped close to Rhodri, holding out her hand. "Ride with me this morning?"

Rhodri took her hand, walking with her from the throne room. The Fae followed, including Dione. Melody stared after them, unable to bring herself to follow as she watched Dione walk from the room, the movement of the eight legs sending a shiver through her.

Chapter Three

By the time Melody could bring herself to move, the throne room was nearly empty. There was a handful of Fae standing around in clusters gossiping, a couple of humans and Brynn. Her gaze was drawn to him chained in the corner. He now sat down, his back against the wall, and as if he could feel her gaze on him, he looked in her direction.

"I wouldn't if I was you."

She turned to see who'd spoken to her, finding a human at her shoulder. He was only a little taller than her, had a scattering of freckles, sandy brown hair and dark blue eyes. "Wouldn't what?"

"Whatever you were planning. Don't feel sympathy for him. He killed one of Dione's knights. If you help him, you won't end up chained next to him. You'll be dead. They've got no reason to keep a human alive."

"I hadn't planned to do anything." She'd been too busy trying to get past the idea of a spider as large as Dione.

"I'm Noah." He held up a violin. "A violinist. What had them inviting you here?"

"I'm Melody." She certainly wasn't going to explain how she'd been forced to repay her mum's debt.

Noah laughed. "Really?"

It took her a second to realise he was talking about her name. She nodded. "Yeah."

"That's cool. Can you sing?"

She shook her head.

"Can you ride?" He gestured in the direction the Fae had taken.

Again she shook her head.

"Pity. No one will teach me. You've got to stay close to the king and queen. That's where everything is happening. If you gain their notice and keep it, no one will bother you. Unless of course the king and queen notices you for the wrong reasons." He glanced towards Brynn.

Remembering Noah's earlier question, Melody asked, "What had them inviting you here?"

"Someone heard me playing at a concert and asked me if I wanted to play for the Queen of the light

Fae. I thought she was joking at first, but when she showed me, I knew this is where I belonged. The Fae worship beauty in all its forms." Again he glanced towards Brynn. "But they're also vindictive, so be careful. You don't want to do anything to anger them."

"Thanks." She'd already known a lot of what he'd said, but it was nice to hear it from someone else. Although she would have preferred to learn that all the stories Elon had told her mum had been lies. "What do you do here?"

"Play my music for the queen."

She felt like rolling her eyes. That much had been obvious. "What else?" There had to be something to do around here other than follow the Fae around. She noticed most of them had left while they'd been talking. There were only two by the door, speaking softly. And Brynn, who was unable to leave.

Noah shrugged. "Join the feasts they have every night."

That was the last thing she wanted to do. The less time she spent with the Fae the safer she'd be. It was going to be a very long time until she was free of the Fae if there was nothing for her to do. She'd worked it out on the ride here. Three-hundred and twenty-three days. She'd be lucky to make it past a week. Even though time didn't pass that quickly here compared to the human world, it was going to feel like forever.

Noah gestured towards the doorway. "I'm going to have a sleep. They don't need as much sleep as we do. You should do the same."

She watched him leave, the other two slipping through the doorway behind him. A look around the throne room showed it was only her and Brynn. She saw he was watching her. She didn't know if that was still or again, but guessed it didn't really matter. Turning her back on him, she strode to the doorway and stood there looking at the corridor that stretched out before her. She had no idea what to do or where to go. If she left the throne room she might never be able to find her way back. And asking wasn't a good idea. She didn't want to risk owing anything to anyone else. Not even for a simple favour. Besides, she didn't want to lose the bet over something so minor.

Turning to face the nearly empty throne room, she again saw Brynn was watching her. Why? Did he want something? Her gaze was drawn to the goblet left by the sword, just out of his reach. Did she dare push it towards him? She thought of all she'd heard. It had sounded like he'd tried to help a human against one of Dione's people. A shudder ran through her at the thought of the arachnid woman. And she'd thought a huntsman spider in her room had been terrifying. Dione was far worse.

She took half a step forward. They were still alone. Several large windows along the walls to her left and right let light into the throne room, but none of them lit up the wall behind the thrones clearly. Slowly crossing the room, she kept glancing around. No one came in and she finally reached the goblet. There was no way she could let him go thirsty regardless of what he'd done. She didn't know what she could do about his hunger. The food in her backpack wouldn't last her three-hundred and twenty-three days. Even taking into account less days would pass in the realms of the Fae compared to the human world.

Keeping an eye on Brynn, she crouched and slid the goblet forward, hoping it was close enough for him to reach it. She stared at him a moment longer, sighing softly when she found herself taking one of the muesli bars from her backpack and placing it beside the goblet. Rising to her feet, she took a step away from him.

He remained against the wall. She turned and started to walk away. Not sure what she could do and not willing to leave the throne room, she headed for one of the windows on the far side of the room. The sound of the chain moving stopped her and she turned to face Brynn.

He stood by the goblet, the muesli bar in his hands as he eyed the packet he'd opened. He raised it to his nose and breathed in deeply. Lowering the packet, he stared at her again. "Don't trust Noah."

"Why?"

He stared at her a moment longer before he spoke. "I'm not sure what you're asking. Why I've told you or why you shouldn't trust him. Or is there another reason for your why?"

"Why I shouldn't trust him." She was pretty certain the offer of the warning was because she'd helped him. It had seemed the most logical explanation, but then again the Fae didn't always seem logical.

"Because he's Eolande's pet and does everything possible to please her." He picked up the goblet and drank the contents before returning it to the floor. He gestured towards it. "You might want to return it to where the queen placed it."

She looked from Brynn to the goblet and couldn't help noticing how little space there was between the two. Even though it felt like a really bad idea, she walked over to him and bent to pick up the goblet. Before she could do anything other than stand, Brynn grabbed hold of her wrist. She tried to pull away, but he was far stronger than her.

"Why help me? It would be your death if you're caught."

She couldn't look away from his intense stare. "I don't know." Her words were quiet and when he leaned closer she thought he might not have heard her clearly.

"You won't last long doing things without reason." He reached out and lifted a lock of her hair, letting the strands drift through his fingers. "Pity." He let go of her wrist.

She didn't step away. "Why?" He smiled and her breath caught. No wonder humans fell prey to the Fae so often. How could they resist such an otherworldly beauty?

"There you go with your ambiguous questions again. Or do you think we can read minds and need but a prompt?" He looked past her. "Someone walks towards the throne room."

It took a couple of seconds for his words to sink in and it wasn't until he moved away from her that she placed the goblet on the floor and hurried to the nearest window to stare outside. She'd wanted to know why he thought it was a pity she wouldn't last long. Hearing someone enter the room, she looked towards the doorway. It was a human. She watched as the man made his way to the thrones and polished them with the cloth he carried, not looking in her direction once. Not even when he eventually finished his task and left the room.

When they were alone again, she looked towards Brynn. He sat against the wall and stared in her direction. There were so many questions she needed the answer to, but even asking them of a chained Fae probably wouldn't be a good idea. He wouldn't owe her that much. Not really. She looked away, not sure what to do. The days were going to pass extremely slow if she was forced to spend them in this one room for fear of losing her way.

The room remained empty and she grew bored enough to finally risk venturing down the corridor, checking the rooms and other corridors she passed. She didn't go far. Not wanting to become lost, she kept returning to the doorway of the throne room. Each time she stood there, Brynn stared at her until she turned and walked away again.

Several times she stopped and took a break from her explorations to sip some water and eat a biscuit. The small amount of food she had in her backpack wasn't going to last her very long. She needed to find running water before she finished all her food and water. She had no idea how she was going to do that if she couldn't find her way out of the castle. A pity there was no GPS here. Or a map.

Late afternoon, humans brought in tables and chairs and set them up in the throne room, covering the tables with embroidered cloths. One long table was set up in front of the thrones, several chairs placed on either side of them. Not a single human looked in her direction. Feeling insignificant, she returned to her explorations, finding a bathroom and a door leading to a walled garden. Wandering around the walled garden had her eventually looking through a window into the throne room. She couldn't see Brynn from this angle, but she could see the humans had now left and Fae were starting to arrive.

She thought about returning to the throne room, but decided to explore the walled garden a little more. She found a water feature, but didn't think it would count as running water. Somehow she had to find naturally running water. There was no way she wanted to get trapped in this place by eating their food.

When it began to grow dark, Melody returned to the throne room. Elon was there and beckoned her to join him where he sat in one of the chairs to the left of the king's throne. Seeing Dione wasn't there, she headed towards him. Her steps slowed as she wove her way through the tables. She didn't want anything at all to do with the Fae. Why couldn't Elon leave her be?

"Where have you been?"

"I can't ride, remember?"

"In future, you remain beside me until I dismiss you."

She nodded, not game to do anything else with the frosty tone he used to speak to her. The sound of a chain moving, had her wanting to look towards Brynn, but she didn't take her attention off Elon.

"You may stand at my shoulder in case I need you to fetch anything." He made a motion with his hand as if shooing her away.

It wasn't until she was standing at Elon's shoulder, and out of his sight, that she looked towards Brynn. He stood at the end of the chain, his sword still out of arm's reach. His gaze was focused on the doorway and he didn't once look towards her. She pushed away the irrational feeling of disappointment. She had to remain detached. No making friends and no getting caught up in this world. The last thing she wanted was to get stuck here. She was going home on her eighteenth birthday. Although she had no idea how she was going to explain to anyone, other than her mum, what she'd been doing for nearly a year. The truth was no good. Not a single person would believe her.

The king and queen arrived and she froze when she saw Dione followed them in, several arachnid people with her. She nearly stopped breathing when Dione walked past her, the sounds of her multiple legs against the floor a sound she'd only heard in nightmares. Even when Dione seated herself several chairs away on the other side of the queen, her people standing at attention behind her, Melody couldn't relax. She only hoped Elon didn't expect anything of her because she doubted she could do more than remain frozen on the spot.

The meal continued for a ridiculously long time and Melody had to force herself not to keep glancing towards the arachnid people. It was impossible to prevent herself every time, but eventually Dione and her people left, following the king and queen from the throne room. Melody blinked several times as she realised Elon was part of the procession leaving the room and she had no idea if he'd dismissed her or not. How could she bring herself to follow him? Even looking at Dione made her freeze. She relaxed a little as the arachnid people stepped through the doorway, tensing again as Elon glanced towards her. The look he gave her had her guessing he hadn't dismissed her.

Chapter Four

Ignoring her mental pleas not to follow, Melody forced herself to hurry after Elon. She was in time to see him disappear around a corner. Managing to keep him in view, not seeing Dione once, Melody caught up to him before he entered a door he left open. She remained in the doorway, taking in the elaborate sitting room, a door off to her right leading to an equally elaborate bedroom.

"You do know how to close a door, don't you?"

She stepped inside, closing the door and remaining beside it.

"I would have thought you'd be more intelligent than this. At least as intelligent as your mother." He dropped into an armchair and gestured towards the bottle of wine on the small table the armchairs were clustered around. There were several glasses with it. "Pour me a drink."

She did as he ordered, spilling a little of the wine on the table. Not seeing anything she could use to clean up the mess, she left it there.

He took the glass of wine she handed him. "Can you do anything other than be an ornament?"

She was tempted to point out that he'd been the one to kidnap her. If it could be considered kidnapping since her mum had made her go with him. She glanced around the room and spotted some bookcases. The familiar spines of her mum's books surprised her. "I can read."

"How clever of you." His tone dripped sarcasm.

Her eyes narrowed. "Out loud. Mum gets me to read out her words when she's stuck on a section she's editing. She says I have a good reading voice."

He waved lazily towards the books. "Go ahead then. Let's see if your mother was telling the truth or was only trying to make you feel like you had some talent, regardless of how insignificant it is."

Her hands curled into fists. She forced them open, not wanting to let him see that his tone, implying she had no talent, had bothered her. After a deep breath that didn't help calm her, she crossed the room and took one of her favourite books from the shelf. Her hands tightened on the paperback and there was an ache in her throat that she tried to ignore. She couldn't show him any weakness. Making her way to one of the armchairs, she sat on the edge.

"What are you waiting for? The king and queen to change their mind about having an early night? I can tell you now, it won't be happening. Everyone is in for a tedious night instead of the night of dancing and partying that we expected."

Wondering what else she'd missed about the night, she opened the book and cleared her throat. It didn't take long to become lost in the familiar passages of the story and she had no idea how much time had passed when Elon rose to his feet.

"Enough. You were passable. Maybe more than a little." He strode to the bedroom door. Pausing, he glanced back at her. "Dismissed." Stepping through the door, he closed it.

She stared at the door, still holding the book she'd been reading from. That was it? She'd survived her first day with the Fae? Rising, she left the book open and face down on the coffee table, away from the spilled wine. Now what? She looked around the room. She supposed she could remove some of the cushions from the armchairs to sleep on.

After she'd created a nest for herself in the corner, she slipped out of the room to try and find the bathroom. Several times she had to backtrack, but she eventually found it and after using it headed towards Elon's sitting room. She started to turn a corner, but froze when she heard someone speaking Dione's name.

"He's alone. Dione wants you to find Fileas and for the two of you to take care of him. Make sure it doesn't look like he was killed by one of our people."

"I could use his own sword on him."

The first man chuckled. "That would be fitting."

Brynn was nothing to her. She needed to stay out of the affairs of the Fae if she wanted to escape on her eighteenth birthday. An image of him standing, staring at her, his hand wrapped around her wrist as he asked why, came to mind. Her shoulders slumped. She had to do something. She couldn't leave a defenceless person, even one of the Fae, to face murderous arachnid people on his own. Not knowing exactly how she could help, she tried to find her way to the throne room.

It was nearly dark in there. Most of the lights, identical to the ones that dotted the ceilings of the hallways, were out. They reminded her of small and distant stars and she remembered them being mentioned in several of her mum's books. Other than knowing they were Fae magic, she had no idea how they worked. She hoped the arachnid people were right and there was no one else in the throne room, hiding in the shadows.

Keeping to the wall, she headed for the far corner where Brynn was chained. She heard the chain move as she came closer and saw his shadowy figure halt as he reached the end of his chain. Nearly standing on the sword, she came to a stop. There was nothing she could do. She had no key. Or even a pair of bolt cutters. Her gaze was drawn to the sword, a glimmer of light reflecting off the hilt.

"Why are you here? I've already repaid you for the bit of sustenance you offered."

She was tempted to tell him he was about to owe her a favour worth far more than food and drink, but she didn't know how much time she had left before the arachnid people arrived. Not knowing what else to do, she slid his sword closer with the toe of her sneaker. At least he'd be armed against them. Remaining near the wall, she headed for the door. She didn't make it in time.

Two arachnid people came into the room, striding towards Brynn. She remained huddled against the wall, hoping they hadn't noticed her.

"I have no argument with you, Fileas. Or you, Pirro."

"That's too bad. We have an argument with you."

Melody recognised it as the voice she'd heard in the hallway so guessed he must be Pirro. She remained pressed against the wall, unable to move. Her gaze followed the movements of the shadowy arachnid people, her heart racing at the thought of them spotting her. Why couldn't she have stayed out of this? It wasn't her fight and Brynn was nothing to her.

"Leave while you can," Brynn warned.

For a second Melody thought he spoke to her, then realised he was talking to the arachnids.

Fileas laughed. "You're chained to the wall, unarmed and there's only one of you. Keep your warnings to yourself. It's you who should be worried."

Picking up his sword, Brynn drew it from the scabbard and tossed the scabbard towards the wall. "At least one of your beliefs are wrong. Last chance to leave before you end up finding out how many more are incorrect."

Fileas and Pirro didn't answer. They drew their weapons and attacked. Brynn retreated and the arachnids leapt around him in the shadowy corner. Melody watched as the sword glinted and glimmered as it caught the limited light. The arachnids used daggers, darting in and out as they tried to get him.

Brynn was too quick and none of their attacks landed. They weren't so lucky. Several times she saw Brynn's blade connect with the bodies of the arachnids. She pressed a hand to her mouth so she didn't accidentally make a noise and catch their attention.

The fight didn't last long and the two arachnids ran through the doorway. She came away from the wall, planning to leave in case they brought more back to finish the job.

"Why did you help me?"

She ignored his question, having no real answer for him, and turned towards the doorway.

"Melody, wait."

She faced him again, wishing she could see his expression.

"Why did you help? I'm nothing to you."

She hesitated. "It didn't seem fair." She spun and fled the room, hoping she didn't run into any arachnid people. Several times she became lost, but she eventually found Elon's sitting room and curled up on the cushions.

As tired as she was, she lay awake for ages, trying to figure everything out. It didn't help. She was still utterly clueless when she fell asleep and in the same state when she woke.

A noise had her sitting up and she saw a human

place a tray of food on the small table and put the wine away in a cabinet. She was almost relieved it was time to get up so she didn't have to endure any more nightmares. At least not until tonight. Several times she'd woken during the night, heart racing and hoping she hadn't called out. Each time she'd listened, worrying that Elon had been disturbed. When everything remained quiet, she returned to sleep. She couldn't remember a single image from any of her dreams, only the sound of a very large spider walking across the floor.

As soon as the human left the room, she returned the cushions to the armchairs. The food looked delicious and she had to force herself to walk away and have some trail mix and water from her backpack. Before Elon came out of the room she took inventory of what she had left. She'd drunk half a litre of water yesterday. Far less than was ideal. She'd also eaten nearly half the packet of sweet biscuits as well as some of the dried fruit and trail mix. Having given Brynn one of the muesli bars, she only had five left. She desperately needed to do something about food and water.

Elon came out of his bedroom, helping himself to some of the food as he headed for the door opening onto the corridor. "Attend me."

She had no idea exactly what that meant, but guessed he expected her to follow him since he didn't pause, but strode along the corridor. She slid her arms into the straps of the backpack before she hurried after him. Did that mean if she hadn't been there for him to say 'attend me', she would have still been dismissed? If only there was someone she could ask. Not that she planned to do anything about it straight away. Hopefully she'd win the bet and get horse riding lessons. Then she might think about staying out of his way for a bit.

By the time they reached the throne room, Elon had finished eating and he made his way towards the thrones. Neither the king or queen were about, but there were plenty of Fae in the room. Her gaze was drawn towards Brynn and she was surprised by how relieved she was to find him alive. He sat, leaning against the wall, his sword back on the floor. She wasn't completely certain, but she thought that where it was he might be able to reach it.

He looked towards her, holding her gaze a moment before he looked away.

She forced herself to stop watching him and checked out the rest of her surroundings. There were still no arachnid people that she could see and she hoped it stayed that way. She turned her attention to Elon. He didn't seem to need her, but he hadn't dismissed her yet. He talked to a woman in a many layered dress that seemed to float around her. Months of following Elon around was going to get boring pretty quick. She was already finding it far too tedious.

Eolande entered the throne room and the crowd separated, creating a path between her and the throne. More Fae trailed in after her. Instead of heading for her throne, she strode towards Brynn, stopping in front of the sword. "Have you learned a lesson, Brynn?"

"Life is full of lessons to be learned, Your Majesty."

"What lesson have you learned from this?"

"Was there a particular one you were hoping I've learned, Your Majesty?"

Eolande smiled. "If only you had displayed such caution when you came across Dione's knight in the forest." She gestured one of her attendants forward. "Set him free. He's been punished enough."

"No!" Dione pushed through the crowd. "Only death is a suitable punishment."

Eolande's smile vanished. "Are you saying you disagree with me?"

The room fell silent and Melody almost felt sorry for Dione. She was surprised the arachnid woman managed to hold Eolande's gaze and not retreat. Elon's frosty tone had been nothing compared to the queen's.

After half a minute of silence, Dione bowed to the queen. "You continue to remain as just as always. My people and I shall soon return to our holdings." She didn't move until the queen gave her a haughty nod.

Chapter Five

Melody watched Dione leave. She was surprised to see Brynn follow her out the door. Someone must've set him free while her attention had been on Dione. She was going to have to stop doing that. She couldn't keep an eye on only the arachnids, there were others to be wary of too.

"Bring me my pet musician." Eolande was seated on her throne.

Noah pushed through the crowd. "I'm here, Your Majesty. What would you like me to play for you?"

"Something melancholy followed by something lively."

Noah stepped to the side of the throne and began to play.

Melody stared wistfully at the door leading from the throne room. She hoped Elon didn't plan to keep her at his side all day. Not if this was all he was doing.

Ages later, the king joined them and a while after that humans circled around the crowd with trays of food and drinks. She had no idea how much time had passed, but she was bored and hungry and wished she could be anywhere other than here.

She spent some time thinking about what her dad might have said when he'd read her letter and wondered what her mum was doing. She thought about friends who had expected her to go places with them during the holidays and wished she wasn't stuck here. She looked around at the crowd. They were beautiful and all of them appeared to be having a marvellous time talking and laughing, but nothing actually seemed to be happening. The stories her mum wrote made the realms of the Fae seem far more interesting. She wanted to go home and couldn't understand why anyone would want to be here.

Her gaze was drawn to Noah, who continued to stand beside the throne playing his music. Was it normal to be able to play for hours without taking a break? He'd been at it for most of the day and he was looking a little ill. Would Elon expect the same of her? To wander around after him unnecessarily, completely forgetting she existed and would need a break.

When he finished talking to the man he currently

spoke to and started to walk away, she stepped up beside him. "Are you finished with me yet? I need to use the bathroom." As well as drink and eat.

Elon looked her up and down. "You are such weak creatures." He slowly shook his head. "Useless and weak. Your mother is much more interesting than you are."

She almost demanded why he hadn't taken her mum instead, but she didn't want that either. "I can't help being human."

He made a flicking motion with his hand. "Dismissed." He turned his back on her and walked away.

She stared after him. It took several seconds before she realised she could go. A smile formed as she hurried from the throne room. After using the bathroom, she found her way to the walled garden and sat on a timber seat tucked away in one of the corners. She finished off the packet of biscuits and tried not to empty one of the water bottles. It couldn't be helped. She was so thirsty. She also had a handful of dried fruit and worried about how little was left of them. Feeling sleepy after her restless night, she curled up in a grassy area nearby, using her backpack for a pillow. There was very little light left in the sky so the dimness of the afternoon and her tiredness helped her fall instantly asleep.

Fear brought her awake and she sat up, eyes wide, checking the area around her. Several metres away from her Brynn sat leaning against a tree. He wore a long sleeved shirt and leather boots with his fitted trousers, his sword at his side. Even with several coloured lanterns hanging in nearby trees she couldn't tell if he was looking at her or not. She was still trying to figure out what to say to him when he spoke.

"What did your ambiguous 'why' mean?"

She struggled to remember what he was talking about, then realised it was when their conversation had been interrupted by the human cleaning the thrones. "Why is it a pity I won't last long doing things without reason?"

"You can't expect answers when you ask such unclear questions."

"I just asked a perfectly clear question and you still didn't answer me."

Brynn chuckled softly. "Answers aren't always given just for the asking."

"Does that mean you aren't going to answer my question?"

He shrugged. "Why did you help me?"

"I already told you. It wasn't fair. You were unarmed and it was two against one."

"What are you expecting in return?"

It was her turn to shrug.

"So you plan to hold this favour over me."

"No, I just don't think you can help me."

"What do you need help with?"

She started to say escaping Elon, but didn't know if that would be too big a favour. It was more that she needed to leave without Elon wanting to come after her than needing to escape. Maybe a map would be useful and then she could find running water. But what if there was no running water on the map? "Naturally running water."

"You aren't planning to stay?"

She shook her head. "I'm only obligated to stay until my eighteenth birthday, next year in the human world."

He rose to his feet and crossed the distance between them, holding out his hand. "Can you ride?"

She took his hand, trying not to growl her reply. Why did everyone have to keep asking her that? "No."

He continued to hold her hand once she was standing. "How long must you remain here?"

"Three hundred and twenty-three human days in total."

"You seem very ill prepared to last that long."

She drew her hand from his grip. "I'll manage." Picking up her backpack, she put it on. She should have known he couldn't help. Walking away from him, she tried to think what else she could do.

"Do you want me to take you to naturally running water?"

She faced him. "I can't ride."

"I can show you, but without being able to ride it's not going to be of much use to you."

She thought of the riding lessons she was hoping to win from Elon. "Okay." When he nodded and walked off, she hurried after him, walking beside him. She tried to take note of the direction they took, but by the time they reached the stables she was hopelessly lost. There was absolutely no way at all she'd be able to find her way back to the throne room. Or even Elon's room. Somehow she'd have to figure it out. She doubted Elon would be pleased if he had to come looking for her.

At the stables Melody watched as Brynn saddled a horse. It was completely black, standing out amongst all the white horses in the stables. She followed him as he led the horse outside and swung up into the saddle. He held a hand out to her and she took it. He effortlessly swung her up behind him. Holding onto him as the horse moved forward, she tried to figure out how he'd managed to sit her behind him so easily. Was it something to do with Fae magic? Elon had done the same. At the time there'd been too many other things happening for her to really think about it. She put the question aside, needing to focus on where they were going.

It didn't take long to realise that she was definitely going to need to learn how to ride. Wishing she had a watch, she could only guess that it took them at least half an hour to reach an orchard, where she dismounted to collect apples, and about another half an hour to reach a stream.

She sat on the bank of the stream and took her sneakers off before rolling the legs of her jeans up. Taking two of the apples, she entered the stream and washed them. How long was it necessary to wash them in running water before it would be safe to eat them? None of her mum's books had mentioned the exact time. She washed them for approximately a minute each. Returning to the bank, she stared down at Bryn. He was sitting beside her backpack and the small pile of apples she'd collected. "Are these safe to eat now?"

"They would have been safe to eat in a lot less time than you took."

Hearing the humour in his voice, she started to tell him there was no need to mock her. She changed her mind. He'd given her not only the answer she'd sought, but the information she'd needed. "Thank you."

It didn't take long to wash the rest of the apples and fill her empty water bottle. She had a long drink from it before refilling it and returning to the bank. She took a bite from one of the apples and held another out to Brynn.

He didn't take it straight away. "You're an odd creature. I can't figure out if it's deliberate or accidental the way you continue to try and keep me in your debt."

"I have no idea what you're talking about."

"That's what I'm beginning to think." He paused a moment. "Why did you offer me this?" He held up the apple she'd given him.

She shrugged. "I don't know. I guess because it's rude not to."

"We're in no one's house. The rules of hospitality don't apply here."

She had no idea what he was talking about. Telling

him he wasn't making sense didn't seem like the polite thing to do. "Okay."

He chuckled. "You have no idea about what I said so why would you agree to it?"

She sighed. Maybe she should have stuck with being rude. He obviously didn't have a problem being rude to her. "Would you have preferred it if I said you weren't making any sense?"

"No, because that wouldn't have been true. You could have said you couldn't make sense of my words."

"That's pretty much the same thing."

"Not at all. What you planned to say was insulting to me."

"So it's perfectly okay for me to insult myself instead?"

Brynn laughed.

She stared at him, wishing there were pretty coloured lanterns hanging from the trees nearby, like there had been in the walled garden. She had no idea why he was laughing, but didn't really care. It was the first time she'd heard him actually laugh. It was a deep rich sound that filled the star studded night with a warmth she hadn't realised it was lacking. When she found herself leaning closer to him, she jerked away.

His laughter faded. "What's wrong?"

"I don't want to get tangled up with any of you. I want to go home on my eighteenth birthday." His laugh had her yearning for things she shouldn't be wanting.

He reached out and captured a lock of her hair, threading it through his fingers. "There's not a chance of any entanglement between us. You're human and I'm half light Fae and half dark Fae. You've seen how easily accusations attach themselves to me. Even a full light Fae would have problems if they took a human lover."

She scrambled to her feet, backing away from him. "I wasn't… I didn't… that is…" Her words trailed off as she felt the warmth in her cheeks. "You lot are all so young looking that you could be a hundred years older than me for all I know."

He chuckled. "I'm barely a year older than you."

The disappointment she felt at not hearing a full laugh from him was replaced by surprise. "Really?"

He rose to his feet. "Really."

"What about Elon?"

"What about him?"

"How old is he?"

"Has no one ever taught you how to ask questions properly?"

His tone annoyed her. Her first impulse was to tell

him not to talk to her like she was an idiot. "Has no one ever taught you how to answer questions properly?"

"I've had plenty of lessons in that. Your Elon is far more than a hundred years older than you."

"Lessons?" She heard weariness in the sigh her words brought and she wondered if she bored him. There was no way she was going to ask him, in case he said yes.

"Are you ready to return to the castle?"

It was her turn to sigh. "I suppose." She gathered the apples and put them in her backpack before sliding her arms through the straps. Rolling down the legs of her jeans, she slipped her feet into her sneakers. When he swung her up on the horse behind him, she couldn't resist asking, "How do you do that?"

"Someone is really going to have to teach you how to ask questions. Yours are far too ambiguous."

She glared at his back as he urged the horse forward instead of answering. The rest of the ride to the castle was silent and when they reached the stables and dismounted, she remained while he unsaddled and brushed his horse. Once the horse was returned to the stall, they walked outside. No one else was around.

"Thank you for taking me to the stream."

Brynn continued to walk towards the castle. "Even

though the destination is of little use to you since you can't ride?"

"I'm working on that." She kept pace with him.

"How do you plan to solve your inability to ride?"

"By winning a bet."

Brynn stopped abruptly and faced her. "If you should lose the bet, what then?"

There was enough light to clearly see his expression, but it didn't help. She had no idea what it meant. She raised her hand. "I lose one of the charms from my bracelet." She didn't plan to lose. She hated the thought of parting with any of her mum's only reminder of the mother she'd lost.

He held her gaze a moment longer before he took her hand and stared at the charms. He slowly turned the bracelet, pausing at each one. Again he met her gaze. "You have so few to waste them on a game of chance."

She pulled her hand from his grip. "I guess I better make sure I don't lose then."

"What were the terms?"

She shook her head, not wanting to share them with him. The terms pretty much showed how little Elon thought of her and her ability to survive in this realm. "I need to return to Elon. I've been gone longer than I'd planned." She glanced towards the castle, still having no idea how to find Elon's rooms.

Brynn nodded, remaining silent. When she continued to stand there, he asked, "Is something wrong?"

She wasn't a hundred percent certain if he still owed her a favour and she didn't want to risk owing him one. Shaking her head, she faced the castle. Surely she could manage to find Elon's rooms. Maybe she could follow any Fae she found until they went to the throne room. She was reasonably good at finding his rooms from there.

Brynn stepped up beside her. "What's wrong?"

She couldn't bring herself to look at him. "What isn't?" She forced herself to walk towards the castle. When Brynn kept pace with her, she glanced towards him several times, but didn't ask what he was doing.

Chapter Six

Inside the castle, Melody wandered the corridors, trying to figure out where to go. Brynn continued to walk with her. Glances towards him eventually became glares and she began to walk faster. He remained at her side.

"You're lost."

She came to a stop and faced him, continuing to glare at him. "No one was thoughtful enough to give me a map when I arrived."

He chuckled. "I dare say that's because there are no maps."

She made a sound of frustration that sounded very similar to a growl, before striding down the corridor. She barely managed not to make the sound again when Brynn walked beside her.

"Why haven't you asked me to show you to where you wish to go?"

Stopping abruptly, she faced him. "Because I-" she broke off when someone came around a corner and headed towards them. Not wanting others to hear the conversation she turned away and began to walk along the corridor again. She glanced in the direction the Fae had come from, but didn't turn that way since it didn't look any better than the corridor she was already in.

"Look up."

She did. It made no difference. She still had no idea where she was or what direction she needed to go in. "Why?"

"Learning the patterns of the lights can help you find your way."

Stopping, she stared at the ceiling and what looked like a random pattern of lights. "I guess they weren't mapped either."

"No. Why don't you ask me to show you the way?"

"Because I obviously don't know the rules."

Brynn frowned. He stared at her a moment then slowly shook his head. "No, I still can't make sense of that comment."

"Do you consider yourself in my debt?"

"Yes."

"How will I know when you're no longer in my debt? Will you tell me? And would you warn me if something I asked of you would put me in your debt? I don't want to be stuck here forever. I want to go home."

"A life is a large debt to repay."

His words were soft enough that she found herself leaning in close to catch them. "Will you tell me when it's paid?" She kept her own voice as quiet as his had been.

"If you made it a requirement I'd be obligated to."

"You don't want me to make it a requirement, do you?"

"It wouldn't make sense for me to give you such an advantage under the circumstances."

Even though it felt wrong, she couldn't stop herself from saying, "I am making it a requirement. I don't have a choice." She couldn't let herself be trapped. Weariness hit her. It was more than being tired and how late it had grown. Thinking about how carefully she would have to watch what she said and did, until she could leave, drained her. "Can you please show me to Elon's rooms?"

He inclined his head then led the way.

She had a feeling he was angry. He didn't speak to her once and he kept his pace fast enough it was a struggle for her to keep up. When he stopped and motioned towards a closed door, she guessed they'd arrived. "Thank you." She reached for the door handle.

"Have you no more orders?"

The feeling became a certainty with how sharp his tone was. She dropped her hand to her side. "I'm sorry." She tried to think of something else to say, but nothing came to mind. She stared at him a moment longer before turning away and reaching for the door handle again.

He grabbed hold of her wrist before she could make contact. "What are you sorry for?"

It took her nearly a minute of confusing thoughts before she figured it out. For having treated him like a slave. She wanted to keep him indebted to her, like some talisman she could pull out when she needed one. But it wasn't fair. She'd chosen to help him. He shouldn't be forced to pay for something he'd never asked for. "You don't owe me anything."

Brynn frowned, continuing to hold her wrist. "How can you be sorry for something that isn't true?"

She grinned. Obviously she was making a mess of this. "I'm not. It's everything else I'm sorry for. All you owe me is a warning so I don't accidentally put myself in your debt."

"You think my life is that insignificant?"

She made the same frustrated growl as before,

pulling away from him. "Unbelievable." She shook her head. "You Fae are going to drive me crazy." She opened the door before he could stop her and slipped inside, closing the door behind her. A glance showed the room was empty and Elon's bedroom door was shut. This was going to be far more difficult than she'd thought. She made her way to the armchairs and began to collect cushions to sleep on. When she finally lay down, she stared at the ceiling and the soft lighting. It had only been two days. What had made her think she could last a week without ending up in someone's debt?

*   *   *

When she woke, feeling surprisingly well rested, she found Elon's bedroom door open and a note from him on the table near the armchairs. 'Attend me when I dine in the throne room tonight.' There were no windows in the sitting room, but she found one in the bedroom. Looking outside she judged it was about midday. She had hours to herself and no idea what to do with them.

After an apple and a muesli bar, she decided it might be a good idea to use the bathroom and wash her clothes. She could hang them over the trees in the walled garden to dry. Who knew when she'd next have the opportunity and it wasn't like she had a limitless supply of clothes. Slipping her backpack on, she crossed the room and opened the door. She froze. Brynn leaned against the wall opposite the door. His long dark hair was pulled back from his face so she could see his slightly pointed ears.

He moved away from the wall. "Do you have plans for the day?"

She shook her head, then nodded.

"Was that a yes or a no?"

"I have to attend Elon when he dines in the throne room tonight."

"That's hours away. Come with me." He held out his hand.

She wanted to take it, but instead curled her fingers up to help resist the temptation. "I can't."

"Why can't you?"

Telling him she'd rather watch her washing dry than spend time with him seemed pretty lame. She needed to be practical. This was only her third day. There were a lot more she still had to get through. "Maybe tomorrow." She stepped out of the doorway and closed the door behind her, heading towards the bathroom.

Brynn walked with her. "We need to talk."

Was that all? Why couldn't he have said that to start with? "I'll meet you at the walled garden in an hour." That should give her more than enough time to wash her clothes and herself.

He nodded and strode off in the opposite direction.

She stood there a moment, staring after him. It wasn't until she reminded herself that an hour wasn't long that she hurried to the bathroom. Worried she hadn't given herself enough time she rushed, reaching the walled garden well before Brynn. She managed to hang her garments over branches and eat two more apples and he still hadn't arrived. She needed a watch and had to figure out something else she could eat. Nearly a year of eating apples would have her thoroughly sick of them before long.

A noise had her turning to see Brynn walking towards her. She rose to her feet, with a glance towards her washing, and walked towards him. "What do you need to talk about?"

He gestured towards her clothes hanging from the branches. "This is what you needed to do?"

She shrugged. "It's not like I have servants to run around after me." She thought of all the humans that scurried around the castle doing the bidding of the

Fae. When he continued to stare at her, she blurted out, "What?"

He slowly shook his head. "Do you truly not understand the way things work here?"

"What things exactly?"

He gestured towards the clothes again. "Why haven't you asked me for someone to serve you while you're here?"

She shook her head, not wanting to get into a conversation that would probably make her feel extremely uncomfortable. How could she possibly order someone around? Not only that, would she be liable for any debts they owed? "What did you want to talk about?"

"Repaying you for the debt I owe."

"I already said there is none."

"And I told you my life isn't that insignificant."

"Don't you people believe in gifts?"

"Of course, but they always come with strings. Some come with ropes and chains."

She turned away from him. Maybe Elon was right. There was no way she was going to survive a week let alone nearly a year. Even if the year passed quicker in this realm. "My gift has no strings and it certainly doesn't have ropes or chains." She walked away from him and sat at the base of a tree, leaning against the trunk. She chose a tree that didn't have her washing hanging from it.

Brynn followed and continued to stand over her, staring down at her. "Why would you do that? What else are you expecting?"

"Do you have to tower over me?"

He sat beside her. "What do you expect of me? My permanent loyalty?"

"Doesn't anyone do anything without expecting something in exchange around here?"

"No. Maybe lovers occasionally, but even that is rare."

It was only by closing her hands into tight fists that she managed not to reach out to comfort him. "I'm sorry."

He frowned, tilting his head slightly. "What are you sorry for this time?"

"Your people. The Fae."

Confusion gave way to surprise and was quickly followed by laughter. "No wonder Elon wanted you for his pet."

She was so caught up in enjoying the sound of his laugh that it took a moment for his words to sink in. "I think he's a little disappointed in the bargain he made."

"Then he's a fool." He reached for a lock of her hair and twined it through his fingers.

"Why do you keep doing that?" She tugged her hair from him.

"What Fae can resist the lure of gold? No matter the form they find it in." He lifted a lock of her hair, letting it immediately fall back to her shoulder. "Come for a ride with me."

She glanced towards her wet clothes. "I can't. My things aren't dry."

"If they were, would you come for a ride with me?"

She shrugged, trying to figure out what he was getting at. It felt like some kind of trick question. "I suppose."

He slowly smiled and the scent of summer breezes and beaches filled the air, a light breeze tugging at her hair. "In that case, gather your gear and let's go."

"What?"

Brynn rose to his feet, pulling her with him. "You agreed to go for a ride with me once your clothes were dry." He gestured towards them.

She looked between him and the clothes several times. It was impossible. She checked her jeans first since they were made of the thickest material. They were completely dry. As were the rest of her garments. She folded them and returned them to her backpack. "How did you do that?"

He chuckled. "How do you think? Do you forget what I am?" He held out his hand. "Are you ready?"

Chapter Seven

Melody didn't bother mentioning that all she knew about the Fae was what Elon had told her mum and she'd chosen to put into her books. She had a feeling it wasn't much at all and probably not anything that was extremely important. Other than the trick of picking her own food from the Fae orchards and washing it in naturally running water. There was no way she wanted to be stuck in this realm because she'd eaten their food. Hopefully she'd be able to find something other than apples, once she learned how to ride. She took his hand. "I need to be back in time for dinner."

He nodded. "You already told me that. The Fae only forget those things they choose not to remember." He continued to hold her hand until they entered the castle.

"Make sure you don't choose to forget." She had no

idea what Elon would do if she disobeyed him, but she didn't think she wanted to find out.

"We'll be back in time."

She walked with him to the stables, trying to remember the way. Like he'd suggested, she regularly looked up, but it didn't help. What was she meant to be looking for in the pattern of the lights? They all looked completely random to her.

This time one of the humans working at the stables saddled the horse and she guessed Brynn had only done it last night because none of them had been around. Today they rode in a different direction and she took note of every landmark. She really needed to know this realm better if she wanted to survive until her eighteenth birthday. And not just survive, but to remain free of debts to other Fae.

The ride took well over an hour and they came out of a forest to see a medieval looking village with a castle in the background. It was a mixture of single and two-storey buildings, mostly made of timber with some stone ones amongst them. The cobblestone road rang out beneath the horse's hooves as they travelled down the main street to stop in front of a tavern.

When they dismounted she tried to ignore the ache in her legs from being on horseback two days in a row. "Why are we here?" She kept her voice low, not wanting any of the humans she could see to overhear her words.

Brynn tied his horse to the hitching post out the front of the tavern. There were two other horses there. "For human food."

"I can eat here? Without being stuck in this realm?"

Brynn nodded.

"Where does the food come from? Who makes it?"

He gestured in a direction different to the one they'd arrived from. "The outlying human farms. They provide some of our food as well, but our cooks mix it with Fae food. The humans of this village make the food." He stared directly into her eyes. "I will never do anything to trap you. I owe you that at least." He gestured towards the front door. "Shall we?"

She nodded. Real food sounded amazing. Inside there were tables of various sizes with stools and chairs around them. A man stood behind a timber bar that took up the far wall, serving drinks to the people seated on the stools along the bar. Brynn headed to a table for two in a less crowded area.

A barmaid wove her way through the tables, a smile on her face as she nodded and chatted to the people she passed. "You haven't been in here for a while, Brynn. Since when have you taken up with humans?"

There was no malice in the woman's words, but Melody still had to fight the urge to argue over them.

"Other matters have kept me busy and had me chained to the castle." He nodded towards Melody. "This is Elon's pet, not mine."

Her humour about his first comment evaporated. She wanted to say she was no one's pet, but it obviously wasn't true, as much as she wished it wasn't.

"What can I get for you?"

"Something a starving man would appreciate. One who has barely had a chance to eat in days. Make that for two."

When the barmaid nodded and walked away, Melody glared at Brynn. "Do you have to tell people I'm Elon's pet?" She kept her voice as low as possible, not wanting anyone to hear her question.

"Aren't you?"

"That's not the point."

"Then what is the point?"

She looked away from his gaze. She didn't have a clue what the point was. Anger turned into confusion and was rapidly replaced with weariness. What had her mum been thinking, making a bargain with the Fae?

"Melody?"

She returned her gaze to him.

"What is the point?"

She shook her head, muttering, "Nothing." She crossed her arms, resting them on the table.

He started to reach for her, but drew his hand away. "Why do you lie so much?"

His question startled her. "Why do I lie so much?" Her tone was filled with disbelief. "I don't."

He nodded. "Clearly something is wrong and yet you said that nothing is. This is why we never trust you humans. You are constantly lying."

She stared at him. "You consider that lying?"

He nodded.

"That's just plain odd."

"What do you call it then?"

She shrugged trying to figure out how to explain it to him. "It depends. Sometimes it's a way of saying none of your business or that it isn't important or it's something that can't be put into words."

"How is one to tell the difference?"

"You haven't had much to do with humans, have you?"

He shook his head. "Other than the occasional meal

here, dealing with human servants and the pets of others, no. I haven't."

She didn't get a chance to say anything else as the barmaid brought two plates over to them. The barmaid was followed by a boy who carried cutlery, a jug and mugs. Melody's gaze followed the plate of roast vegetables and sliced meat topped by a dark gravy as it was placed in front of her. It took all her willpower not to snatch the cutlery from the boy and devour the food.

The moment the barmaid had poured wine into the mugs and walked away, Melody started to eat. The food tasted divine and she hoped it was because she hadn't eaten a proper meal in three days and not because it was enchanted Fae food. Once they'd eaten, the barmaid returned to clear away their plates and bring apple pie with a dollop of cream on the top. Melody ate it as quickly as she'd eaten the roast meal, taking sips of the wine since she didn't want to drink so much that she was tricked into some agreement. She would like to be able to trust Brynn, but she couldn't let herself completely trust any Fae. The risk was too great.

Once the meal was over, Brynn left a handful of coins on the table and gestured for her to precede him to the door. Outside, instead of riding, he led the horse as he walked towards the forest in the direction of the light Fae castle.

"How do people earn money around here? Or was that enchanted money that will turn into leaves after we've left?"

"We aren't allowed to use trickery on the humans within their village, by orders of the king and queen. They've been given sanctuary here. If they wander away from their village, farms and the parts of the forest that are safe for them, then they're fair game."

He hadn't exactly answered all her questions. Was that deliberate? She wanted to be able to come here again when she learned how to ride, but there was no point if she couldn't afford to buy a meal. "How do people make money here?"

"All the usual ways including war and trickery."

That hadn't helped at all. She didn't know what all the usual ways were for the Fae. Giving up on trying to get an answer out of him she walked quietly beside him. They reached the forest and continued to walk, late afternoon light not penetrating the trees very well. "You aren't planning to walk all the way back to the castle, are you?"

"No, I didn't think you'd want to ride so soon after eating."

She didn't particularly want to get back on the

horse at all, but she also didn't want to be late. "Although my legs will probably hate me for it later, I'd rather ride than be late to dinner."

He stopped and faced her, wearing the frown she seemed to regularly cause. "What an odd turn of phrase. Why will your legs hate you?"

She couldn't help giggling at his confusion. "They're aching from being on a horse for so long today and yesterday. I guess they're going to feel worse by the time we return to the castle."

Brynn dropped the reins and reached for her, wrapping his arms around her. "Why didn't you say something earlier?"

She opened her mouth to protest how he held her even as she fought the urge to wrap her arms around him. The scent of summer breezes and beaches filled the air, a warm, gentle breeze seeming to curl its way around her body. When it disappeared the aches were gone from her legs. She started to ask him how he'd done it then remembered his earlier reply. He was Fae. She couldn't let herself become entangled with him and his life. Drawing away from his arms, she took a step back. "Thank you."

He nodded once and picked up the reins. "Do you wish to ride now?"

"I suppose." The thought of returning to the castle

and leaving his company held no appeal, which meant it was even more important for her to return.

"Was there something else you want to do instead?"

She started to say no, then remembered his question about lying. "I need to return to the castle."

When he was in the saddle, he held out a hand and swung her up behind him. She smelt the feint hint of beaches, more the scent of salt than anything else. Had he used his magic to help her onto the horse or did the smell of it still cling to him from earlier? She wrapped her arms around his waist, not bothering to ask. She doubted he'd answer. They were halfway through the forest when howling came from nearby, immediately answered by several more howls.

"Hold on tight. The wolves plan to hunt."

She tightened her arms about him at the urgency in his voice, pressing herself against his body. The horse felt like it took a leap forward and the trees rushed past them, the hooves pounding on the dirt path. Behind her she could hear snapping and snarling and couldn't resist looking. Her jaw dropped as she stared at the pack of wolves chasing them. She closed her mouth with a snap and faced forward. All plans to travel here on her own evaporated. The ones in the lead had been about three quarters of the size of the horse they rode. Large fangs had been visible and powerful muscles had driven them forward. She wanted to tell Brynn to go faster, but instead tightened her grip.

They burst out of the forest and a few of the larger wolves came out from amongst the trees to watch them, howling at their escape. Melody stared at the wolves as they left them behind, relieved they weren't about to leave the forest and chase them all the way to the castle.

The horse slowed, but she didn't release her grip. "What were they?"

"Wolves."

"But they were so big."

"That is the size of wolves in this realm."

She shuddered, momentarily tightening her grip on Brynn. Would being able to ride help if there were creatures like that wandering around outside the castle?

"Are you fine?"

"I will be."

When they reached the stables, Brynn left his horse with a stablehand and showed her to the throne room. She'd asked him to take her there instead of Elon's rooms because she was worried about being late. He left her well before the doorway to the throne room, gesturing ahead, before leaving her alone. She stared after him, thinking she hadn't had a chance to thank him like she'd planned. Mentally shrugging, she headed for the throne room.

Chapter Eight

Elon spotted Melody before she reached him. He sat at the table to the left of the king's empty throne. He looked displeased and Melody wondered what she'd done wrong. She'd arrived before the king and queen so surely she wasn't late.

"When I leave something for you to wear you'll take it as an order. Return to my sitting room and dress appropriately." Elon's gaze was drawn to her backpack. "And leave that tacky bag, that you insist on wearing everywhere, behind."

"I haven't been in your sitting room. So I didn't know there was a dress."

"Where have you been?"

She shrugged. "About. I spent most of my time getting lost. A map would be nice."

"I can't believe how useless you are. Fae are

superior to humans in every way. Now go and dress and don't take all night about it."

Biting back a retort, she strode from the throne room. She managed to find her way to Elon's rooms without getting lost. The dress was a shimmering bronze with a fitted bodice and a flowing skirt. She stared at it. Never before had she seen anything like it, let alone worn a garment so exquisite. What sort of strings would come with a dress like this? She wanted to refuse to wear it, but Elon's tone had clearly stated that defying him would be a really bad idea.

Having no other choice, she took off her t-shirt and jeans and slipped on the dress. The material clung to her and shifted with her movements. She ran a hand hesitantly over the material. No wonder the Fae could entice humans into their realm. She tightened her hand into a fist and closed her eyes, trying to remind herself of everything she loved about her own world. For some reason Brynn kept coming to mind and causing all the other images to disappear.

Opening her eyes, she jammed her own clothes into her backpack and put it in a corner out of the way. This wasn't her world and she didn't want to remain here as someone's pet. She strode back to the throne room, hesitating in the doorway when she saw the king and queen had arrived. The table was full and her gaze travelled along it, stopping when she saw Brynn seated several chairs away to the right of the queen. What was he doing there? He spoke to a man on his left, nodding his head. He looked away and his gaze turned in her direction. He stared at her for nearly a minute before he looked away and talked to the man again. She looked at him a moment longer before she forced herself to cross the room and stand at Elon's shoulder.

The meal seemed to last forever and she was glad Brynn had taken her to the tavern earlier. Several times she looked in his direction, but not once did she catch him looking towards her. She heard violin music and checked behind the thrones to where Noah stood near the wall, playing soft music. He appeared more fatigued than he had yesterday. Hadn't he ever heard of the word 'no'? He was going to kill himself trying to please Eolande. And she wouldn't care. If anything she'd probably be annoyed at the inconvenience he caused her in needing to get a new pet.

She had to remain detached and not even consider making friends with any of the Fae or the humans who worshipped them. Her gaze was once again drawn to Brynn. She dragged it away and tried to focus only on Elon. He was speaking to the Fae seated beside him, gossiping about people she didn't know. Her attention wandered and her thoughts again drifted back to Brynn. Why had he taken her to the tavern today? She'd told him he owed her nothing. Didn't he believe her?

The Fae rising to their feet startled her from her thoughts. What was going on? They were laughing and smiling and heading to an area in front of the thrones that had been cleared of tables. She followed Elon, guessing he hadn't dismissed her. She was really going to have to start paying more attention to everything that was happening. If only they weren't so boring to listen to. Maybe it wouldn't be that bad if she knew who they were talking about, but she only knew a handful of people in this realm.

Someone took hold of her hand when she reached the area in front of the thrones and bodies pressed in against her. Everywhere she looked she saw the Fae. Glittering creatures dressed in their finest, a few humans amongst them, including Noah clutching his violin. Eolande and Rhodri were in the centre of the crowd and held each other like they were about to dance. The crowd pressed in towards them and Eolande threw back her head and laughed, calling out that the fun was about to begin. The scent of roses filled the room. The world shimmered and reformed itself as the Fae spread out and Eolande called for music.

Melody's hand was released and she stared at the world she could see past the Fae. There were humans, a playground and a star filled night. Familiar stars. She could clearly see the Southern Cross and knew she had to at least be in the Southern Hemisphere. Apart from that, she wouldn't have a clue where she was.

She watched as various Fae approached humans and pulled them towards those dancing around Noah, who was frantically playing his violin. Elon was lost in the crowd and she hoped he didn't complain to her later that he hadn't dismissed her. She eased her way through the crowd, heading for some humans who'd stopped to watch the party that she guessed must have appeared out of nowhere to them. How did the Fae explain that to humans? Or did they leave their magic to deal with any problems?

She reached the side of a boy who seemed mesmerised by the beautiful people laughing and dancing not far from him. "Excuse me." She had to say it twice before he noticed her.

"Are you with them?"

She nodded. "You'd be better off staying clear of them though. There's some very nasty people amongst them."

"I don't like to dance yet ever since I heard that music I've wanted to join them."

Hearing the wistful tone in his voice she wondered if she should be telling him to run. "Where are we?"

"What?"

She smiled wryly, doubting that he'd believe the truth. "It's been a continual party for days. Where've we ended up?"

"Rockhampton."

She was a long way from home. "Do you have a phone I can borrow? I need to call my mum."

He gestured towards the noisy crowd, more humans joining the revelries by the minute. "Why aren't you over there?"

"Please? I won't be long. I just need to let her know I'm okay."

"Do you know that lady?" He pointed to one of the Fae spinning around at the edge of the crowd, her head thrown back and the streetlights making her jewellery glitter and sparkle.

Melody didn't have a clue. "Sure. Why's that?"

"Can you introduce me to her?"

She met his gaze and saw he was already lost. "Only if you promise me not to eat anything they offer you."

He nodded, handing her his phone.

She didn't know if he'd keep his promise, but she'd tried. She looked at the screen of his phone, shocked to see the date. It was eleven o'clock on the twenty-fourth of January. Nearly a week had passed in the human world while only three days had gone by in the realms of the Fae. If only time would continue to pass that quickly, but she knew from her mum's books that it was erratic.

"Are you going to make your call?"

She nodded, dialling her mum's number before the boy changed his mind about her using his phone. She listened to the phone ringing and hoped her mum would answer. How many times had she missed answering a call because she'd been so busy writing she hadn't noticed it ringing?

"Hello?"

"Mum."

"Where are you? Are you okay? Elon hasn't harmed you?"

"Rockhampton. I'm okay and they're all here. Even Eolande and Rhodri."

Sherry breathed in sharply. "Stay away from them. Whatever you do, don't catch their attention."

"I'm trying not to." She looked at the boy. He appeared to be completely focused on the Fae. "I've had some help, but I don't know how much I can accept."

"Don't accept any help. Stay away from all of them as much as you can."

She could hear the fear in her mum's voice. "I don't have much choice. The closest running water is about an hour's ride away. Why didn't you make me take riding lessons?"

"You were never interested."

"How is Dad taking my disappearance?"

"Blaming me."

"Sorry."

"Oh Melody, you've nothing to be sorry about. This is all my fault. I never should have made that bargain, but at the time I was desperate."

The boy turned towards her. "You said you weren't going to be long."

"I have to go. I'll try and call you if we go somewhere suitable again." She was conscious of the boy listening in.

"Be careful. I love you and miss you."

"I am. Love you too." She disconnected the call and, while the boy's attention was caught by the Fae again, she cleared his phone call history. She held the phone out to him. "Thanks."

"Will you introduce me to her now?"

She nodded, not bothering to ask him his name, and grabbed hold of his hand to tug him towards the Fae who fascinated him. The Fae stopped to look at them when they came close. "He would like to dance with you." She pushed the boy towards the Fae who grinned and reached for him.

"Of course you do." The Fae laughed as she held his hands, whirling away with him.

Melody watched them go, wondering if the boy would be as lost as Noah.

"Do you want to join them?"

She turned to find Brynn behind her, his hand held out. "Is it safe?"

He grinned. "Is anything?"

She shrugged, staring at him a moment longer before she placed her hand in his. He drew her close, spinning her around with him. Her arms wrapped around him the way his wrapped around her. The night became a whirl of sound and light. They were surrounded by laughter, frantic violin music, singing and calls to the humans to join in. There was also a mixture of smells that she doubted were normally found in this park and guessed it was probably from Fae magic. Particularly the ones that reminded her of rainforests and flower gardens.

She met Brynn's gaze, the world around them

becoming a blur. It felt like it was only the two of them and the scent of summer breezes and beaches washed over her. Tightening her arms around him, she pressed closer to him, still holding his gaze with her own.

"Did you want safe?"

It took her a moment to figure out what he meant and all of a sudden she couldn't have cared less about safe. She opened her mouth to say no, but his lips met hers and she lost the chance to speak. One of his hands remained against her back while the other threaded through her hair at the nape of her neck. She clutched at him, returning his kiss until someone pulled her away.

Elon glared down at her before turning to Brynn. "She's mine."

Chapter Nine

Melody stepped between them, facing Elon. "It's my fault. I got caught up in the party. Where did you disappear to? If you expect me to follow then you shouldn't move so fast. How's a human meant to keep up with you?" She knew she was babbling, but she didn't want anything to happen to Brynn.

Elon ignored her, looking past her to Brynn. "Wasn't toying with one of Dione's knights enough danger for you?"

Brynn started to speak, but she interrupted, terrified by the threat she heard in Elon's voice. "Why did you bother bringing me if you were going to walk off and leave me on my own? What was I meant to do? Sit around and be bored? Of course I found someone to dance with. And how was he meant to know that you think I'm yours? None of you Fae pay much attention to us humans. You probably think we all look the same."

Elon finally turned his attention to Melody. "You will stop talking if you know what is good for you."

"You promised not to harm me."

Elon reached out, dropping his hand on her shoulder and tightening his fingers. "There are others who might."

Fear rushed through her and it took a lot of effort to continue to hold his gaze.

"If you ask another to harm her it would be the same as harming her yourself," Brynn said.

She felt like groaning when Elon turned his attention from her to Brynn. Why was he still standing there? She wanted to tell him to go before Elon did something to him. There was no way she could do that without letting Elon know she not only knew Brynn, but also cared about him. Far more than she should.

"Did I ask you to interfere?" Elon demanded.

Melody dreaded that frosty tone, but not as much as she feared Elon doing something to Brynn. How could she repay him for the meal he'd bought her this afternoon by letting Elon hurt him? She turned her back on Elon, his hand continuing to grip her shoulder. "You can go now. I'm not alone anymore.

Thanks for keeping me company until Elon found me." She begged him with her eyes to leave.

"That is what you want?" Brynn asked.

She smiled brightly. "Would I lie to you?"

He frowned. "Probably."

Maybe that hadn't been the best choice of words. She sighed heavily. "Just go away. I plan to dance with Elon." Another bright smile and she turned her back on Brynn, hoping he did the sensible thing and left. "Well?"

"I hope you can dance better than you do most other things."

So did she. "I guess we're about to find out." She held out her hand and Elon released her shoulder to take it, leading her through the crowd. As soon as Elon's attention was off her, Melody looked over her shoulder to see Brynn continued to stand there watching her. 'Go, please.' She mouthed the words before she faced forward, not wanting Elon to catch her gazing after Brynn.

They reached the centre of the crowd, not far from the king and queen, and Elon turned to face her. Dancing with him wasn't anything like dancing with Brynn and she was glad when he eventually grew bored with her and turned to a woman who interrupted them. She stood still amongst the dancing crowd, feeling completely out of place. She was surrounded by magic and all she wanted to do was go home. There was something seriously wrong with her.

She caught a glimpse of Noah through the crowd. Sweat dotted his face and there was an unnatural pallor to his skin. Maybe it wasn't her that had something wrong with them. She thought about moving away to the edge of the crowd, but she noticed Elon regularly glanced in her direction. Hopefully the night would end soon and she could get back into her own clothes.

Continuing to look around at the crowd, she spotted Brynn. He danced with a Fae woman who was nearly as tall as him. Every time he faced her direction, his gaze met hers. She wanted to tell him to stay away, that Elon wasn't anyone he wanted to mess with. Not according to the stories in her mum's books.

When Eolande and Rhodri laughingly called their people close, telling them it was time to return home, Melody was relieved. She pressed in close, not wanting to be left behind and cause Elon to come looking for her. The world shimmered around her and reformed. They were back in the throne room.

The Fae started to leave, still talking and laughing,

Eolande and Rhodri amongst the first to go. Unable to see Brynn anywhere Melody hurried after Elon, following him to his rooms. Even though she was tired, her feet ached and she was nearly falling asleep where she stood, she wanted to change into her own clothes. She couldn't find her backpack anywhere.

Elon had already entered his room after saying she was dismissed and shut the door behind him. Too bad. She wanted her gear. She banged on his door.

He flung it open, dressed only in his fitted trousers. "This better be important."

She barely glanced at him, fleetingly thinking he didn't look over a hundred years old. "Where's my backpack?"

"You don't need that ratty thing. I've provided more suitable clothes for you."

She opened her mouth to demand he return the backpack, but closed it instead. Yelling at him wouldn't help. She needed to be smarter than that. Use the trickery the Fae liked to employ. "You promised not to harm me. You need to return it."

"Taking your bag from you doesn't hurt you."

She nodded. "Yes it does. It causes mental anguish, which is a type of harm. And you were the direct cause of it. I want my things back."

Elon's gaze narrowed. "Do you really want to push me on this?"

She thought of her clothes, food and water. Especially the water bottles. "I have to. You made a promise to me and you're breaking it already."

Elon glared at her. "Your things will be returned in the morning." He slammed the door shut.

Melody took a deep, shuddering breath. What had she done? But it had been important. How could she survive without her things? She stood there several more minutes before she gathered cushions from the armchairs and curled up on them to sleep. Exhaustion had her falling instantly asleep and she didn't wake until after Elon had left for the morning.

She found another note from him on the table, her backpack beside it. 'Attend me in the throne room for dinner. Dress appropriately.'

She really hoped it wasn't going to be a repeat of last night. Although she had appreciated being able to call her mum. She reached for her backpack to check everything was still in it. All her things seemed to be there and she opened a bottle of water. Pausing with it at her lips, she wondered what Elon would do to pay her back for her defiance. She held up the bottle and stared at the liquid. Was there any way to find out if her food and water had been tampered with? What if Elon was using this opportunity to trap her in this realm forever? He probably wouldn't consider that as harm. She put the lid on the bottle and shoved it in her backpack. She couldn't risk it.

Not knowing what to do for the day and having no way of finding Brynn or getting to the stream on her own, she decided she'd go to the walled garden after she changed her clothes. Taking out the clothes she'd washed yesterday, she noticed the scent of summer breezes and beaches still clung to them. She held them to her face and breathed in deeply, closing her eyes.

Last night came vividly back to her. Being wrapped in Brynn's arms, the rest of the world receding and the kiss. Everything had been perfect until Elon had interrupted. She forced the memory away, telling herself it had been far from perfect. Getting involved with one of the Fae would be dangerous. She couldn't let herself be caught up in this world. That would be utter madness.

Not knowing if or when Elon would return, she took her gear to the bathroom to change. She jammed the dress into her backpack, not caring if the action ruined it. She headed for the walled garden without losing her way. Her excitement at finding her way there without any problems disappeared when she realised Noah was in the garden. She tried to remind herself it wasn't her garden and he'd probably been using it long before she'd arrived, but it didn't help. She was hungry, thirsty and not interested in being sociable. Socialising seemed to come with too many minefields around here.

Noah broke off playing when he saw her. He lowered his violin and stared at her.

Her momentary feeling of needing to apologise was quickly replaced by annoyance. If she didn't own the walled garden, then neither did he. "What was that you were playing?" She struggled to think of something else to say when he remained silent. Telling him he looked terrible probably wasn't the best topic, even though he did. "It was nice." If you liked melancholy music.

"It's something I've been working on for the queen. Do you think she'll like it?"

How was she supposed to know? She managed to keep that sharp comment to herself, shrugging instead. "I don't really know her. I've only been here four days." Well, technically three because this day wasn't that far along.

"Did you see the cello player one of the other Fae brought along last night? Do you think Eolande was paying more attention to him?"

Was that why he looked so terrible? Eolande was

growing bored with him so he was overdoing things to keep her attention. "I didn't notice him. I only heard your music and the queen wasn't that far from me."

His expression brightened considerably. "Are you sure?"

She really hoped he wasn't going to expect her to tell him what Eolande thought. She had no idea how the minds of the Fae worked and if the conversations she'd had with Brynn were anything to go by, they didn't know much about how the human mind worked either. "Yours was the only music I could hear."

Noah grinned. "I could play it for you and you could tell me what you think."

She gestured towards a grassy area under one of the trees. It wasn't like she had anything else she could do. "Once I get comfortable." When he nodded, she sat down. A pity she hadn't thought to bring one of her mum's books to read. He started to play and setting her backpack beside her, she leaned against the tree, closing her eyes. The walled garden was filled with music and her yearning for home intensified. Opening her eyes, she caught a glimpse of Brynn leaving the garden. Jumping to her feet, she slung on her backpack smiling at Noah who came to an abrupt stop. "I have to go. There's something I forgot to do." She ran towards the exit, glancing over her shoulder. "It was good. I really liked it. I bet Eolande will too."

In the corridor she looked in both directions, trying to find Brynn, who was already gone. She felt like screaming. If it hadn't been for Noah's presence he probably would have come in and talked to her. She guessed all she could do was search for him. After an hour of looking, or what felt like an hour, the only thing she'd managed to do was get herself lost. Some more wandering around had her stepping outside with no way of finding the throne room, or any other castle location she knew. She decided she might as well walk to the stream, even though she didn't know if she could get there and back before she was meant to attend Elon. She needed to eat and drink if she wanted to live.

By the time she reached the orchard, it took all her willpower to prevent herself from eating the apples she gathered, having first got rid of the ones that were still in her backpack. She was so thirsty that even the thought of eating an apple didn't cause saliva to form in her mouth. Ignoring the lure of the apples in her backpack, she forced herself to continue to the stream. When she reached it she found Brynn. He was sitting on the bank, his hair damp and wearing only trousers.

Hunger, thirst and a long walk had put her in a bad mood so she glared at him when he rose to face her. "You lot need phones. How's anyone supposed to get hold of anybody when they need them?"

"Why would you need to get hold of me if as you say I'm not obligated to you?"

She growled in frustration, about to tell him he was an idiot. That it had nothing to do with obligation. "Oh, forget it." She strode to the edge of the stream and took the two bottles of water from her backpack before dropping it on the ground. Kicking off her sneakers, she placed the bottles on the edge of the bank and rolled up her jeans before she waded in with one of the bottles.

Chapter Ten

Standing in the stream Melody tipped the water out of the bottle and rinsed it well before she filled it, doing the same with the other. Taking a long drink she felt a little better, or at least not as thirsty.

Once she'd washed all the apples she sat beside Brynn, who'd seated himself beside her backpack during the process, and took a bite of one of the apples. The sweet flavour burst in her mouth and her stomach growled. She glanced towards Brynn a couple of times. He remained silent, warily watching her. When her apple was half eaten, she smiled wryly. "Sorry." She took another bite.

"What are you apologising for?"

She finished her mouthful. "I shouldn't have snapped at you. None of it was your fault." She stared at him a moment. "I saw you. At the walled garden.

Well, I saw you leaving. I tried to find you, but I ended up getting lost."

"Is that what you were blaming me for? Getting lost?"

She shook her head. "I wasn't actually blaming you for anything. It was more that you were there and I was angry. Although I was probably more thirsty and hungry than angry."

He gestured towards her backpack lying between them. "Why didn't you eat and drink?"

"Because Elon took it from me and I don't know if any of it is safe. I've tried to keep it with me all the time, but it's hard."

"Why did you need to find me? Was it to bring you here?"

"No, well not exactly." She grinned. "I wouldn't have said no to a lift, but I mainly wanted to know if you were okay. That Elon didn't do anything because of last night."

"You don't need to protect me. I'm able to protect myself far better than you can protect yourself. Why do you keep wanting to put me in your debt?"

She sighed heavily. "I don't. At least I'm not deliberately trying to. He's promised not to harm me so I thought it'd be better for me to take the blame.

Everything I've read about him tells me he's very vindictive."

"Read about him?"

"He's been telling my mum stories for years and she's been writing them down and getting them published."

"So your mother is his pet too."

"No." It didn't bear thinking about.

"I've heard talk about his pet author who's been chronicling his life. I've also heard people say he only tells her the stories about his victories." His lips curved into a smile. "Maybe someone should share some of the other tales with her."

Fear arrowed through her and she grabbed hold of his hand. "Don't. He really would come after you then."

He looked at her hand that held his before meeting her gaze. "Why does that bother you?"

It shouldn't. She let his hand go and rose to her feet, taking several steps away and keeping her back to him. It really shouldn't. "Get yourself hurt, see if I care."

He chuckled, stepping in front of her. "You're still lying to me." He reached for her.

Melody threw herself at him, twining her arms around his neck, her lips meeting his. She knew she should push him away, but couldn't bring herself to do it. When she did eventually draw back from him, she held his gaze. "Don't do anything crazy."

"I'm fairly certain it's too late for that warning." He continued to keep his arms around her.

"I don't want you to get hurt."

"You're the one at greater risk than me. You don't even know if you'll have food and water each day."

"I managed to walk here, didn't I?"

"What about the return journey?"

She shrugged. "I guess it would have been pretty similar to the walk here. Cursing Elon every step of the way."

"Would have? Does that mean you're expecting me to return you to the castle?"

She grinned. "No, it means that if you don't I'll be alternating between cursing you and Elon."

He laughed. "I guess we can't have that in case your curses work."

She stared up at him, still caught in the sound of his laughter.

He met her gaze, humour replaced by a look of intensity. His arms tightened around her a moment before his lips met hers again.

They spent the rest of the afternoon by the stream and Brynn eventually took her back to the castle with plenty of time for her to get ready for dinner. He'd told her the sealed packets of food would be fine to eat, but if she wished to be safe she should get rid of everything else. He walked her to the walled garden where she'd asked to be taken so they didn't risk running into Elon.

The garden was empty and he kissed her, pressing something into her hand when he pulled away from her. She stared at the spirals of the small shell. "What's this for?"

"Speak my name against it and I'll know you're looking for me. If it's urgent, crush it after you speak my name."

It looked delicate. "What if I accidentally break it?"

"It's stronger than that. You'll have to stamp on it to crush it."

She slid the shell into a pocket of her jeans. "Why?"

He smiled, raising an eyebrow.

She grinned, remembering his comment about her ambiguous questions. "Why are you giving me this?"

"Because some entanglements form regardless of how much you wish to prevent them." He held her gaze a moment before striding away.

She watched him leave, wishing there was time to ask him more questions. There wasn't. She needed to find out what Elon expected her to wear tonight. She slid her fingers into her pocket, to brush them against the shell, before she headed to Elon's rooms. She was nearly there when she heard a familiar voice. Slipping back into the corridor she'd stepped out of, she peered around the corner at the retreating figures of Fileas and Pirro. A shudder went through her and she was so focused on their spider legs that it took a moment for their words to sink in.

"How smart can he be? Elon said he left the stink of his magic on her clothes," Pirro said.

Were they talking about Brynn? That was the most logical conclusion. Her first urge was to warn him. Her second thought was that she had nothing to actually tell him.

"How did he manage to trick even Eolande into thinking he couldn't reach his sword?" Fileas asked.

Pirro shrugged. "It was probably her doing. He's always been a favourite of hers. Or at least his father is. That was probably why she left it there in the first place. It was only rumours that had everyone thinking she was telling him she could take what she wanted from him and he couldn't do anything about it." They went round the corner, disappearing from view.

Melody leaned against the wall. There was no mistaking it had been Brynn they'd been referring to. She'd have to warn him. She fingered the shell in her pocket. Later. She didn't have time to do it now without defying Elon. She pushed away from the wall, running the rest of the way to Elon's rooms. She nearly ran into him as he stepped out the door.

He eyed her up and down. "Where have you been?"

"I went for a walk."

"Let me guess. You got lost."

She ignored the derision in his tone. "Only a little. I'm sure I'll know my way around here in a month or two." She expected to be able to find her way around much sooner, but she wasn't about to let him know.

"That long," he sneered.

She refused to let his tone bother her. She grinned. "I know, great isn't it?"

Another look of disgust and he strode away.

Still grinning, she entered the room, closing the door behind her. The grin faded when she saw the dress he'd left on the armchair. She remained frozen against the door, her gaze on the black dress with a silver thread running through it. The colours weren't what bothered her. They were actually pretty great. It was the pattern. It looked as if some spiders had spun their webs all across the dress. Did he know? She remembered her mum's warning. How could he possibly know? She'd done nothing to give herself away. Or at least not said anything. Or was this a test? She forced herself to step further into the room.

If this was a test she couldn't let herself fail. Somehow or other she had to bring herself to wear the dress. Even picking it up took a lot of effort and she hoped the Fae had no way of planting listening or recording devices. They'd never once been mentioned in any of her mum's books. It was only by closing her eyes that she managed to pull on the dress. She had to keep herself from looking down otherwise she remained frozen on the spot, her gaze glued to the webs covering her body. Even continually reminding herself they weren't real didn't help. She knew the webs weren't real, but that didn't slow the race of her heart. There was a drawstring bag that went with the outfit and black high-heeled boots. Luckily only the boots had the spider web pattern. She slipped the shell into the drawstring bag, which she hung from her wrist. Taking a deep breath she slid her arms through the straps of the backpack, not willing to leave it behind.

She could get through this night. There was no way she was about to let Elon know she was terrified of spiders. He was sure to find a way to use it against her. She slipped her fingers into the bag hanging from her wrist, rubbing the shell, wondering if Brynn would be there. If the arachnid people were correct and he was a favourite of the queen, then he probably would be. Maybe she'd have the chance to warn him sometime after the meal.

Staring at the door, she tried to convince herself to leave the room. It took a few more minutes before she managed to do so. The corridors were empty and when she arrived in the throne room, which had been set up for dining, she went to stand at Elon's shoulder like always.

She couldn't help checking to see if Brynn was at the table. He was. Her fingers rubbed against the shell as she stared at him seated several seats past Eolande. He looked in her direction, held her gaze for a moment then returned to the conversation he was having with the woman seated at his side. How had he known she was looking at him? She thought of the shell. Could he tell when she touched it? If that was the case, it was extremely unfair.

The sound of music starting drew her gaze to Noah, who was near the wall behind the thrones. The song he played sounded like the one he'd been practising that afternoon. He continued to play throughout the meal, not stopping when the Fae rose from the tables and humans cleared them away for dancing.

Elon looked her up and down. "What do you think of your gown?"

Almost certain this was a test, she held his gaze for a moment, before she looked down at herself, keeping her gaze unfocused. "How could anyone not find such a dress beautiful? It's like the moon is highlighting the webs on a dark night." She was surprised she managed to say the word 'webs' without stumbling over it. She met his gaze again to find him still staring at her.

"That is surprising."

"Why? Don't you like it? If you didn't like it, why did you choose it?"

He glanced towards Noah who continued to play. "I was told you might be scared of spiders."

"Really? Whatever would make someone think that?" She had to be more careful around the arachnid people. Preferably by not being anywhere near them.

"Your expression each time you saw Dione or one of her people."

Melody forced herself to laugh. "My expression was probably one of disbelief. I didn't know creatures like that even existed." Why would Noah say something to Elon? She hadn't done anything wrong to him. She'd even listened to his stupid music this afternoon.

Elon laughed. "Maybe you aren't as brainless as I thought. There are many who believe the Demi Fae belong in the Fringes along with the rest of the misfits and exiles. You're dismissed."

Chapter Eleven

Elon strode off before Melody could ask him what the Fringes were. She knew the Demi Fae were all Fae that weren't light or dark, including ones that were part human, but she'd never heard about the Fringes. If he'd ever told her mum where exiles were sent, she'd never put it in her books.

She absently rubbed the shell as she surveyed the room. Numerous Fae were dancing while others stood around talking and laughing. Eolande and Rhodri danced past her and a woman kept pace with them.

"Why not give your protégé a break? You should listen to mine play his cello. You'll want to dance all evening," the woman who kept pace with them said.

Eolande nodded. "Organise it. If your pet fails to live up to your words he'll be banished from my court."

"You won't regret taking the time to listen." The woman hurried off as the king and queen danced away.

Melody watched the woman beckon to a young man with a cello. He crossed the room in her wake as the woman made her way to Noah. Unable to hear what was said, Melody guessed it hadn't been anything Noah had liked if the way he glared at the woman and strode towards the door was any indication.

She hurried after him, wanting to find out why he'd said something to Elon. She caught up with him in the corridor. "Noah, wait."

"What?"

"Why did you tell Elon I was scared of spiders?" She was extremely impressed with how she managed to keep her tone even. She'd drawn the shell from the bag and held it in her hand. It was starting to feel like the worry stone one of her friends had given her a couple of years ago. She'd lost it within a week. She doubted she'd be so careless with the shell.

Noah took a step away from her. "Why would he tell you that?"

"Because he's annoyed you're wrong."

"I saw you."

She shrugged. "What did you expect? It was like

watching some creature that had escaped from a horror movie I was watching in 3D." He looked confused. "How long have you been with the Fae?"

"Time is different here."

"What year did you leave the human world?"

"1943."

She stared at him. "Seriously? How old were you back then?"

"Nineteen."

He didn't look a day older. All thoughts of spiders fled her mind as she struggled to accept what she'd only read about in fiction. Knowing and seeing were obviously two different things with how difficult she was finding accepting his words.

"What?"

"You don't sound like you're from that decade."

"I like to learn what's going on in the world. I can't say anything I've heard or read makes me miss it." He shrugged. "It was always full of big promises it never kept. Look at the war to end all wars. Did it? Obviously not."

She didn't want to get into a discussion with an old man, no matter how young he looked, about the state of the world. She'd experienced enough of those conversations to know it would only bore her. "Why did you tell Elon? What did I do to you?"

"You lied to me."

It was her turn to feel confused. "When?"

"You told me you liked my music and then ran from the garden. Why lie about it?"

She felt like laughing. The type of laugh one gave when they were confused, surprised and just plain dumbfounded. And she'd thought she'd been nice to him. "I got so caught up in your music I forgot I was meant to be elsewhere. I ran because I was late and you don't keep the Fae waiting." No wonder Brynn was always telling her she lied. Before coming here she hadn't needed to. Other than the occasional white lie to spare someone's feelings or politely leave a conversation she didn't want to be a part of.

"You did? You were?"

"Yes."

"Oh."

When he remained silent, she felt like saying 'now what'. Was that all he was going to say?

"What are you planning to do?"

"About what?" He'd obviously been hanging around the Fae too long. He was almost as hard to understand as one of them.

"Are you going to retaliate?"

"Ahh." She smiled. "No, but if I was wouldn't it be stupid to warn you?"

His shoulders slumped. "So you're going to retaliate."

She felt like kicking herself. She should have left her comment at 'no'. "Why would I do that? Because of your comment Elon gave me this gorgeous dress." She smiled, forcing herself to touch the material, her other hand still closed around the shell. "Maybe you could tell him I'm terrified of kittens. I've always wanted one of them."

"I doubt he'd believe me now." He gestured towards her dress. "Not after that failure."

Good. She shrugged, keeping her smile in place and her tone light. "Pity."

He looked past her. "If my song was as good as you said, why did Eolande let the cello player take my place?"

"She didn't. Not exactly. It was…" she trailed off, thinking that using the word 'owner' probably wasn't the best choice. "A woman who said he was her protégé convinced Eolande to let him play. The queen said if he didn't play in a way that had her wanting to dance all night then he'd be banished."

"Really?" Noah's eyes lit up. "Banished?"

She nodded.

"I have to go." He strode towards the throne room. She stared after him for a moment, pitying the cello player. She probably shouldn't have said anything. She couldn't even manage to reassure someone without them taking it the wrong way. With a slight shake of her head, she made her way to the walled garden. Rubbing the shell, she wondered what Brynn was doing. Passing the windows that looked into the throne room she kept her gaze away from them. She didn't want to know if he was dancing with other people and enjoying himself. She reached the far corner, thinking she should have stopped at the bathroom and changed out of the dress. Looking around, she tried to find somewhere private she could change, but even though the corners were secluded, there were none that were completely private.

"You look beautiful."

She spun to face Brynn, her hand tightening on the shell. "I hope you're not saying that because of the dress. I don't plan to wear it ever again. I should have changed into something else before I came out here."

"What's wrong with it?" He reached out to trace a section of the pattern.

She opened her mouth twice before she managed to think coherently. "Elon heard I was scared of spiders and wanted to find out if it was true."

"Is the rumour true?"

Even to Brynn she couldn't bring herself to say she

was. Instead she told him about her encounter with Noah.

"Are you planning to retaliate?"

She shook her head. "No."

He had moved closer during her tale and now ran his fingers through her hair. "Do you want me to retaliate on your behalf?"

"No."

"It's safer to retaliate than to let others think they can get away with harming you."

She shrugged. "Maybe. But that's not me."

"No wonder I worry you won't last until your eighteenth birthday."

She grinned. "Yeah, I will. I'll just keep lying my way through all my problems and somehow I'll get home at the end of it."

"Are you sure you'll want to go home when you turn eighteen?" His hand stilled in her hair.

She held his gaze, the colour of his eyes looking strange from the light cast across his face from the blue lantern hanging nearby. "I can't stay. I don't belong here." Her words were soft and more difficult to say than she'd expected.

"No entanglements."

It took her a moment before she could nod.

"You don't sound as certain as you did only days

ago. How certain will you be in a month? Or two months?" He lowered his head. "Or when all the days have passed and Elon releases you from your obligation?" His lips met hers.

She wrapped her arms around him, still holding tightly to the shell, all thoughts of answering gone. When they eventually drew apart, she struggled to recall what they'd been talking about and remembered instead the arachnid people she'd overheard in the corridor. She told him about the conversation. When he said nothing in return, she asked, "Aren't you worried?"

"No. They'll continue to retaliate for some time yet. You should be careful though since Elon is involved."

"He promised not to harm me."

"Elon has been around for over a century. I'm sure he could find a way around it if he really tried. Make sure you don't anger him enough that he tries."

"It looks like I'm not the only one he's angry with."

He reached out and brushed his fingers across her lips. "I don't blame him."

She rubbed the shell she still held, trying to think of a reply. When he glanced at her hand, she remembered her earlier thought. "Do you know when I touch this?" She held up the shell.

"Only if you're also thinking of me." He grinned. "I should have given it to you sooner."

She glared at him. "That's not fair. It's not like I can give you one." She paused. "Or can I?"

"Not unless you have the ability to wield Fae magic."

"How do you get to do that?"

"The easiest way is to be born Fae."

She thought over his words. "So there are other ways?"

"Weren't you planning on leaving this realm as soon as you can?"

She nodded "Yes. I can't survive here forever." She thought of all the problems she'd already encountered. How could she survive a lifetime of them?

"Then you have no need of Fae magic."

She absently ran her fingers over the shell again, stopping when he glanced towards her hand. "It's not deliberate. I've started doing it when I'm thinking."

"Of me?"

She grinned. "Partly. I had a worry stone some years ago and I guess this has now taken its place. Let's hope I don't lose it like I did my worry stone." She doubted she would. The worry stone hadn't been important to her.

When she eventually returned to Elon's rooms, it was to find his door closed and the lights in the sitting room dim. She guessed he was already asleep. After she changed out of the dress, she sorted out a place for herself to sleep in the corner, and curling up she fell instantly asleep, still holding onto the shell. There was no way she was going to lose it.

A sound woke her what felt like minutes later and she opened her eyes to see Elon close the door that led into the corridor, walking quietly to his room. He shut the bedroom door behind him. Melody stared at his door. Where had he been and why had he left the place looking like he'd already retired for the night? She thought of how he'd been plotting with the arachnid people earlier and wondered if he was working on more plots. Rubbing the shell she hoped Brynn was okay. A pity it didn't work like a phone. The Fae needed technology. Things like phones and GPS. Did they have anything like that? In a magical sort of way? Drifting off to sleep again, she made a mental note to ask Brynn tomorrow.

When she woke the next morning it was to find Elon gone and there were no orders left for her. After using the bathroom, she checked to see if anyone was in the walled garden. It was empty and she sat in the far corner eating an apple and a muesli bar for breakfast.

Once she was finished, she stared at the shell, turning it in her hand as she tried to decide if she should call Brynn. A shadow fell over her and she looked up to see him standing there, smiling. She grinned. "I was just thinking about you."

He chuckled. "I know." He held out his hand. "Do you want to take a ride with me?"

"Where are we going?"

"The tavern we visited two days ago."

She took his hand. The food she'd eaten had barely taken the edge off her hunger. "That could easily become my favourite place."

Chapter Twelve

The way to the stables seemed a little more familiar and Melody silently tried guessing the direction before Brynn took it. She managed to get it right about three quarters of the time. Which wasn't too bad, but it still meant she'd have been lost on her own.

On the way to the tavern, she asked, "Why is your horse black?"

"It was a gift from my mother."

"And?"

He glanced over his shoulder. "That is a very open ended question. What information in particular were you looking for?"

"All of it?"

Brynn laughed.

Her arms tightened around him and she wanted to find more ways to make him laugh. How could she resist such a sound? "Why don't you just answer the question you think I'm asking and if you get it right I won't need to ask a second one?"

"Why don't you ask the question you want answered and I won't need to tell you unnecessary information?"

"Is any information unnecessary?"

They reached the tavern and he remained silent until they'd dismounted and tied the horse to the hitching post. He met her gaze. "No."

It took her a few seconds to realise what he was answering and she had to hurry after him since he was entering the tavern. "Then why are you so stingy with it?"

"Because you don't toss it away like it has no value."

She thought about his words while he talked to the same barmaid as last time, finding herself worrying at the shell she drew from a pocket of her jeans.

"You do that a lot." His gaze lowered to the shell before returning to her eyes.

She shrugged. "I was thinking about what you said. It's an odd way to look at things."

"Would you throw away all your valuables?" He gestured towards her charm bracelet.

"No, but…" she tried to think of how to put her thoughts into words. "It would be like throwing away money. The answers I'm looking for aren't that valuable."

"Aren't they?"

"Well, not all of them are." She paused. "Are you trying to tell me I need to pay for information?"

"No. I'm trying to figure out why you need some of the information you seek."

His words surprised a burst of laughter from her. "You and me both." At his frown, her grin widened. "It's mainly curiosity."

He inclined his head. "But what will you do with the information you gather with your curiosity?"

"Most of it, nothing. Once my curiosity is satisfied then I can stop wondering about whatever it was I wanted to know and think about something else."

"So if I wanted you to think about me more often I shouldn't answer so many of your questions."

Her eyes narrowed. "That's mean."

"No, that's logical. You were the one who gave me the information."

"But it wasn't-" She broke off, her mouth rounding in surprise. It had been far more valuable than she'd realised. "Did you do that deliberately?"

He smiled, nodding towards the barmaid bringing their food, the same boy trailing behind her. "Food has arrived."

She waited until they were alone again. "Did you do it deliberately?"

"Why do you need to know? Are you planning revenge if I did?"

"I should be, but no. I want to know."

"Yes. It was deliberate."

"Thank you."

"What are you thanking me for?"

"Helping me figure out something I should have already known." She thought of Noah telling Elon about her fear of spiders. What had he hoped to gain from that other than revenge? He'd been with the Fae long enough by now that he was sure to think more than a little like them.

"All knowledge is valuable, even more so when you realise how it can be used."

She nodded. That was what she needed to do. Learn everything possible, even the boring stuff. It might be something that would help her survive until her birthday. Slipping the shell back in her pocket she ate the food. It was a meat pie with a flaky pastry, vegetables on the side. After the main meal was finished the barmaid brought chocolate cake topped with berries and cream. Once they'd eaten, Melody reluctantly left the tavern with Brynn.

On their ride through the forest, she leaned against

Brynn, her arms loosely around him, the horse at a walk. "I really need to learn how to ride."

"Why do you need to?"

"Because this is the first time I've felt full since the last time you brought me here."

"What horse do you plan to ride?"

She swore. "I hadn't thought about that." Everything was far more complicated than she'd thought it would be. "Aren't there any horses I could borrow from the stables?"

"No, they're all owned by someone. If you tried to ride one without permission it would throw you. That's if you actually managed to get on its back. You also shouldn't travel through the forest alone. There are more than wolves looking for prey."

She tried not to feel disappointed, but it was difficult. Especially since this was the fifth day of her bet. She was so close to collecting on it. There had to be some way of getting hold of a horse. "Why didn't you warn me against going to the stream on my own?"

"I wouldn't say it's completely safe in that direction, but it's far safer than this one. There's no wolves."

"Why?"

He laughed softly.

"Fine. Why are there no wolves?"

Instead of answering, he stopped the horse. "Get off. Quick."

Hearing the urgency in his voice, she didn't argue. "What's wrong?"

He pressed her against three large trees growing close together and held out a silver dagger. Leaning in, his lips brushed against her cheek. "If something should happen to me, stay here until they're gone and stab one of the trees with the dagger. Then ask it to release you in my name." He pulled away from her. "Don't move." He touched his hand to the closest tree and the scent of his magic filled the air.

Melody opened her mouth to ask him what was happening when arachnid people dropped out of the trees behind him. Before she could move forward to help him, the trees lowered boughs and grew woody shoots enclosing her in a cage. "Brynn!"

He spun, drawing his sword as he raced forward to attack the closest arachnid knight. There were four of them, all armed with daggers. "I will fight to the death. Do you really wish this to be your last day?"

Melody stared at the arachnid people, who continued to attack, recognising only one of them. Pirro. He was the only one who looked uneasy at Brynn's words. She clutched the dagger in her hand

and hated how she couldn't help. Not only could she not fight, but the thought of getting any closer to the arachnid people made her heart race and her limbs freeze.

One of the arachnid people laughed and he leapt forward, blades slashing. "You should be the one worried it's your last day."

Brynn blocked him. "Sorrow!" His horse reared up, slashing out at a nearby arachnid knight with his hooves.

Melody watched through the gaps of her tree cage as all the arachnid knights attacked at once. She clutched at the tree, desperate to do something, not having a single clue how she could help. The arachnids managed to get in several strikes that drew blood, while Brynn stabbed one of them through the chest. He darted in and out of range of the arachnids and she half expected him to sprout wings with how high he sometimes leapt. When he killed a second, the other two ran through the trees. Brynn gave chase, stopping before he was completely out of sight. He turned to face her and Melody gasped at the blood she saw on him, some of it so dark it was nearly black. Obviously it wasn't all his, but she still worried about how badly he'd been hurt. She raised the dagger to use on her cage when it began to open.

The moment there was a large enough gap, she squeezed through it and ran to him. She tried not to look at the bodies as she passed them. "Are you okay?" She started to reach for him, stopping with her hand outstretched at the thought of possibly hurting him further. The thought of coming into contact with all that blood also wasn't pleasant. "I mean, I know you're hurt, but well…"

"I'll live." He glanced down at himself. "But I certainly need a wash. I can't return to the castle looking like this."

"We could go to the stream." She lowered her arm.

He nodded. "Do you want me to leave you at the castle first?"

"No."

"When do you need to attend Elon?"

She shrugged. "He didn't say. I have no idea where he is." She held out the dagger. "Here."

"Do you have a weapon of your own?"

"No, but it wouldn't do me any good. I have no idea how to use one."

He stared at her a moment before taking the dagger and looking past her. "Sorrow. Here." The horse trotted over to them and he swung up into the saddle.

"Why did you call your horse Sorrow?" She took

the hand he held out to her so he could swing her up behind him.

"I didn't."

"Who did?" She gingerly held onto him as the horse moved forward.

"My mother's father."

"Why?" After a short pause, she hurriedly added, "Why did your grandfather name the horse Sorrow?"

"The horse was a gift when my mother left her people to be with my father. Her father wanted her to remember how he and the rest of her family felt about her leaving."

"Oh." She fell silent, not knowing what else to say. The fact she'd had a fairly normal conversation after seeing a battle and two creatures dying made her feel odd. Shouldn't she be doing or saying something else? All she felt was relief that Brynn was still alive and worried about where the arachnid knights had gone. Did they plan to return with reinforcements? If they had no further plans for today what about tomorrow and the days after?

Brynn glanced over his shoulder at her. "Are you fine?"

"Yeah. I wasn't the one fighting." She fell silent for several minutes. "When will they stop?"

"When enough of them die that they feel it's not worth losing more."

"What if…" When her voice failed, she cleared her throat. "What if it's not one of them who dies?"

"I don't plan to die."

"But what if they send twice as many next time?"

"I'll send for some of my knights tomorrow. Dione's people will stop when they know they'll have to face several knights to kill me. I would have sent for them sooner, but I hadn't planned to stay here this long."

"You have knights? Where are they?"

"In my castle."

She opened her mouth several times, but not a single word came out. He had his own castle? It wasn't until they were passing the orchards she finally managed to speak again. "How did you end up with a castle? You're not much older than me."

Brynn chuckled. "It's in my care. It's part of my family's holdings. My parents live in the main castle while my brother and I live in two of the smaller castles."

"Oh." She guessed his family must be extremely wealthy. She was tempted to ask how many castles they owned, but didn't think she really wanted to know. Did owning a castle make them royal? She wracked her brain, trying to remember what was in her mum's books. No, it only made them one of the nobility. Which meant they were important in the Fae world. Far more important than a human pet.

Chapter Thirteen

The rest of the trip to the stream was silent and after leaving her backpack on the bank, Melody joined him in the water to wash off the blood she'd got on herself from sitting behind him. Standing on the bank once they'd washed, she checked him over, finding several minor cuts and two deeper ones that still bled a little.

Brynn reached for her and the scent of his magic filled the air. "I'm sorry I brought my troubles to you."

She felt her clothes and body dry and guessed it was Brynn's doing. "I've got a feeling I added to them by agreeing to dance with you." She wrapped her arms around him, resting her head against his shoulder. "What are we going to do about it?"

"We will do nothing."

"But they'll keep attacking."

"I'll deal with it. You will stay out of it. You've already told me you can't fight. That's all I can do for now. At least until my knights arrive."

"But–"

"No. Promise me you won't get caught up in this. Aren't you the one who said no entanglements?"

She drew away slightly to glare up at him. There had to be some way she could help.

"Promise me."

She wouldn't stay out of it forever. "I promise to give you a chance to deal with it before I think about getting involved."

"Not quite the promise I was looking for."

She shrugged, smiling slightly. "That's all you're going to get."

He smiled. "That was a very Fae promise."

She was both pleased by his compliment and horrified at the thought of becoming more like the Fae. "We should go back to the castle before it's dark." Already the day was nearly ended. She didn't want to be out here after dark and unable to see any creature that might be coming their way. Particularly one of the arachnids.

"At least promise me not to become involved for three days, no matter what happens. That should give me enough time to contact my knights and for them to arrive."

A lot could happen in three days. Look at all that had happened since she'd arrived and it was only the fifth day. "I'll give you one day."

"That's a promise?"

"Yes. I promise."

"You do know you can't break a promise to the Fae."

The scent of his magic filled the air and she immediately wanted to take her promise back. She'd known promises to the Fae were binding, but she was beginning to think they were a lot more unbreakable than she'd thought. "I know."

He inclined his head before turning away and swinging up into the saddle, holding out his hand.

After slipping her arms through the straps of the backpack, she let him help her onto the horse.

By the time they arrived back at the castle, it was dark and Brynn left her not far from Elon's rooms. She found them empty with no new dress for her to wear or a message. Not knowing what else to do, she made her way towards the throne room. Before she reached it, Noah caught up with her. She tried not to show her annoyance. All she wanted to do was make sure Elon didn't need her so she could retreat to the walled garden and eat a couple of apples for dinner.

Noah held out a small gold charm in the shape of a violin. "I noticed your bracelet and thought you might like this as a thank you."

"Thank you for what?"

"Your kind words yesterday and also to apologise for what I said to Elon." He still held out the charm.

It seemed excessive to her. She slipped her fingers into her pocket and brushed them against the shell, thinking of Brynn. "Which words in particular?"

"All of them."

She still didn't take the charm. "It's very pretty." She looked at the charm he continued to hold, her fingers brushing against the shell as she continued to think of Brynn. Maybe if she thought of him for longer than usual he might check on her. Would it be too obvious if she brought out the shell and whispered his name against it?

"So you accept it?"

She frantically tried to think of a reply, still thinking of Brynn.

"What an interesting trinket." Brynn reached past Melody and took the charm from Noah.

Melody almost sagged against him in relief.

Withdrawing her fingers from her pocket, she remained in place.

"It's a gift for Melody," Noah said.

"What strings are attached to this gift?" Brynn asked.

"This is a private matter between Melody and myself."

His refusal to answer Brynn worried her further. She smiled, trying to keep her concerns hidden. "It's an apology and a thank you for what I said to him yesterday. Nothing major." She was glad she'd told Brynn about her encounter with Noah. Hopefully he'd have a better idea than her what to do.

"Oh? What did you say to him that has him thanking you so profusely?" Brynn asked.

Melody opened her mouth to speak, but Noah interrupted. "She complimented my music, amongst other things."

She suddenly realised what he was thanking her for. "There weren't that many other things. Apart from a misunderstanding, I only mentioned what Eolande said about a cello player."

Noah cleared his throat, shifting from one foot to the other. "I was very grateful to hear what you thought about my music."

"Is that the cello player that was banished today?" Brynn asked.

Melody glanced from Brynn to Noah. "He was? What happened?"

Brynn kept his gaze firmly on Noah. "I'm sure Melody would be willing to accept this trinket as a small measure of what you owe her for the help she's given you and the trouble you've caused her." Brynn held the charm out to her when Noah nodded jerkily. She took it and Brynn gave a shallow nod to each of them before continuing towards the throne room.

"What is Brynn to you?" Noah asked as soon as Brynn was out of hearing.

That was the last question she wanted to answer. She held up the charm. "Thanks for this. I'll put it on my bracelet later." She slipped it into one of her pockets and gestured in the direction of the throne room. "I should see if Elon is in the throne room. If he's there I'll need to attend him."

"I saw him leaving the castle with Dione earlier. She's returned, but I don't believe he has."

She shrugged. "I better check." Striding towards the throne room, relieved Noah headed off in a different direction, she wondered what Elon was up to. For all she knew he and Dione were old friends, but she couldn't help thinking it was more than that.

When she reached the throne room, she froze in the doorway.

Brynn was surrounded by Fae knights and Dione was demanding his death. She wanted to race forward and protest, but couldn't move or speak. For a moment she thought it was her fear of spiders keeping her from confronting Dione and her people, but it felt like more than that. The hint of summer breezes and the salty tang of beaches rose around her as she tried to force herself forward. She remained rooted in the doorway.

"I'm getting quite sick of this fight that's going on between the two of you," Eolande said.

"I don't have an issue with him. He's the one who keeps killing my people. Another two today. When will you put a stop to this?" Dione demanded.

"Yet he keeps saying it's your knights who are attacking him," Eolande said.

"I have two knights who say he attacked them without provocation. Is there anyone willing to stand up and say different?" Dione asked.

Melody felt like crying tears of frustration. Why had he made her promise? She withdrew the shell from her pocket and thought hard of Brynn, willing him to release her from her promise. He looked in her direction for a moment before returning his gaze to the two women arguing about him. Nothing changed. She was still unable to move or say anything.

"I can't see why this has become an issue. Surely your knights aren't so inept that four of them can't protect themselves against one of my knights," Eolande said.

"Are you saying he's doing this on your behalf?"

"Of course not. I have no fight with you." Eolande turned to her knights. "Chain him up again."

"No!" Dione tried to reach Brynn through the Fae knights, but two separated from the group to stop her.

"Do you disagree with my punishment?" Eolande's tone was frosty enough to bring snow to summer.

"Of course not, Your Majesty." Dione's words were forced through clenched teeth. With a gesture towards her people, she strode towards the doorway.

Melody shrank back out of the way. Pirro gave her a look as the group passed. She stared after him. He knew she'd been there. What did he plan to do? And why hadn't he said anything to Eolande about her being there? Or had something been said before she'd arrived? Once the arachnid people were out of sight, she was able to move again, this time it had been fear that had kept her frozen. She peered through the doorway, her gaze drawn to Brynn chained in the corner.

They'd taken everything from him except his fitted trousers, leaving his sword on the floor out of reach. He looked straight ahead, his arms crossed over his chest. She rubbed the shell, thinking as hard as she could about him, even whispering his name against it. Nearly a minute passed before he finally glanced in her direction. He returned to staring straight ahead. She wanted to demand he look at her. Demand he free her from the promise. Instead she spun on her heel and marched to the walled garden, returning the shell to her pocket. The garden was empty. Finding a secluded corner, she sank onto the grass. What was she meant to do?

Not a single idea came to mind. The moment she was free of her promise then she'd do something. She ate an apple and one of the tins of spaghetti while she tried to figure out a plan. Had he contacted his knights yet? She could ask him tonight after the throne room was empty. If he hadn't, maybe there was a way for her to contact them.

She moved closer to one of the windows and watched the Fae dine. She fell asleep while waiting, not waking until after the room was nearly full of shadows. Peering through the window, she tried to see if anyone was in there. A large spider scurried across the window and she stumbled back with an indrawn breath.

Her gaze remained on the spider that stayed in the top corner of the window. It looked to be about as large as her outstretched hand and was as hairy as a huntsman spider. She tried to look away, but was unable to do so. Sliding her fingers into her pocket, she touched the shell. Brynn needed help and standing here staring at a spider wasn't it. She managed to take several steps back from the window. Drawing in a shuddering breath, she again tried to look away from the spider. When it scurried down the window to the opposite corner she turned and fled.

In the corridor, she leaned against the wall, her hand pressed to her heart. Luckily no one was about to see her cowering there. She had no idea how long it was before she could bring herself to walk to the throne room. She stood in the doorway, unable to breathe. There had to be hundreds of spiders scattered throughout the room, as well as webs spun in corners and between the two thrones. The spiders were all shapes and sizes.

The sound of a chain moving caught her attention. But it didn't help. Her gaze darted from spider to spider and she became light headed. Taking in an uneven breath, she backed away. There was absolutely no possibility she could enter the throne room. As soon as she was far enough away, she turned and fled to Elon's rooms.

Closing the door, she remained leaning against it as she tried to empty her mind of the spiders she'd seen. It was impossible. They remained clearly in her mind and likely to give her nightmares. What could she do? It was ridiculous. They were spiders. Something she could squash beneath her shoe. She shuddered at the thought. Maybe someone else could, but she certainly couldn't.

She staggered across the room, gathering several cushions as she passed the armchairs. There were no messages and Elon's door was shut. Which as she'd learned, didn't mean anything. Using her backpack as a pillow, she lay down and drew out the shell to clutch it tightly. She couldn't stop thinking about Brynn chained up in the throne room with all those spiders.

Chapter Fourteen

Sleep was broken by nightmares and every time she came awake she squeezed the shell and tried to convince herself to go and see Brynn. No matter what she told herself, she couldn't return to the throne room. Eventually she gave up trying to sleep and wandered out to the walled garden. It was early morning and she had it to herself. She stared at the windows of the throne room, unable to look away from the spiders scattered across them. It took several minutes for her to escape to the far corner of the garden, where she couldn't see the windows clearly.

She regularly forced herself to check on the windows and it wasn't until the Fae started to arrive that the spiders scurried away. That was worse. She couldn't relax and kept checking to see if any of them had come outside. She didn't see any, but there were plenty of hiding places.

She spent the day in the walled garden, eating the last of the chocolate bars and the rather crumpled box of crackers. By the time night fell, she was down to one bottle of water and would have to walk to the stream tomorrow. She checked in Elon's room and finding no messages from him made her way to the throne room. Where was he? Had something happened to him? If he died or disappeared, did that mean she was released from her obligation? She had no idea and there was no one to ask. Sliding her fingers into her pocket she brushed the tips of her fingers over the shell. Not until Brynn was released.

Pausing in the doorway of the throne room, she saw Elon wasn't there. Nor were the king and queen. Dione and several of her knights stood in front of the table that had been placed before the throne. Checking the room carefully, she couldn't see a single spider or web. She came into the room, staying close to the wall. Her gaze remained on Brynn and even though she touched the shell, focused on him and whispered his name against it, he didn't look in her direction.

The sound of the king and queen entering the throne room drew her attention and she watched as they made their way to where Dione stood. She bowed when they stopped in front of her.

"Your Majesty, as always, you are right. This matter has gone on long enough. I won't complain if you wish to release your knight."

"You're satisfied he's been punished enough," Eolande said.

"I had no cause to raise my voice at you yesterday when I demanded Brynn's death, Your Majesty. My grief over losing more knights overwhelmed me. Can you forgive me for my lapse in judgement?"

Melody wanted to tell Eolande not to be fooled. Dione hadn't said she was satisfied.

"I can understand grief. Haven't we all lost those we care about?" Eolande turned to gesture two of her knights forward. "Release him." She faced Dione again, smiling. "Let us feast." She turned towards the thrones, Rhodri at her side. "We must have music."

Melody wanted to run to Brynn. Instead she continued to remain pressed against the wall, her gaze drawn between him and the arachnid people. When he headed towards the doorway, she forced uncooperative limbs to take her from the room. Did he notice Dione hadn't agreed she was satisfied he'd been punished enough yet?

Brynn didn't glance towards her as he strode from the throne room, holding onto his sheathed sword. No one else was in the corridor and she wanted to ask him if he was okay. She followed him at a distance, her fingers brushing against the shell. Not even then did he look towards her. He eventually entered a room, leaving the door open. She hovered in the doorway, not sure if she should enter. It was a similar set up to Elon's with a sitting room and bedroom.

He faced her. "Come in and close the door. No point in giving the gossips more to talk about."

She did as he said. "You should never have made me promise not to help."

"It was probably the most sensible thing I did."

"Why?"

He smiled faintly.

"Oh, come on. That question wasn't in the least bit ambiguous."

"You would have rushed in there and got yourself killed." He strode to his bedroom.

She followed, about to argue that she wouldn't have. Coming to a halt in the doorway, she watched as he took clothes from a wardrobe and crossed to a closed door, opening it up. She caught a glimpse of a bathroom and wondered why he had his own bathroom when Elon didn't.

He half turned to her with a smile. "Were you planning on joining me?"

She shook her head, her fingers sliding into her

pocket to brush against the shell. As soon as she realised what she was doing, she stopped, turning away from him so he couldn't see the colour that filled her cheeks. Behind her she heard a door close and she wandered over to one of the armchairs and, dropping her backpack on the floor, sat in it.

While she waited, she looked around the room. It was similar to Elon's sitting room. There were different books in the shelves and the colour scheme contained a lot of blue while Elon's had a lot of green, but other than that, she could have been in the same room.

Brynn came out of his room and she rose to her feet, checking him over. "Are you okay?"

He nodded, stopping in front of her and wrapping his arms around her. "Are you fine?"

She held onto him tightly. "Yes."

"I saw you last night. They terrify you, don't they?"

She looked away. "I couldn't enter the throne room. Even when everyone was gone and I wanted to come in and be with you, I couldn't. I'm sorry."

"Noah was right, wasn't he?" He pressed lightly under her chin until she lifted her head enough to meet his gaze.

"Yes." She couldn't manage anything more than a whisper.

He crushed her to him, his lips meeting hers. Eventually he drew back slightly. "Don't leave the castle on your own and if you see one of Dione's people run in the opposite direction."

She frowned. That had sounded like a farewell. "Are you going somewhere?"

"Do you think you can find your way back to my rooms?"

She thought about it. "Yeah, I think so."

He let go of her to take her hand and draw her towards the door, pressing her hand against the doorknob. "Only you and I will be able to open this door." The scent of his magic filled the room. "Even the servants won't be able to come in here now."

"Are you going somewhere?" She stressed the words, needing an answer.

"I'll make sure there's food and drinks here for you." He let go of her hand and pulled her back towards him.

Placing her hands on his chest, she pushed away from him, keeping them there so he couldn't come close. "Brynn."

He lifted a lock of her hair, threading it through his fingers. "It's not safe for me to stay here. I'll gather my knights and return to you. I'll be gone three days, four at the most."

She slid her arms around him and buried her face against his chest, desperately trying not to beg him to stay. He was right. It wasn't safe for him here. Dione was planning something and she needed him free to be able to put it into action. "I'll miss you."

His arms tightened. "Be careful while I'm gone. I hate to leave, but it's the most practical plan."

She couldn't help thinking about him chained up in the throne room last night with all the spiders. "I know."

"I need to gather some supplies for you. Will you wait here until I return?"

"Yes."

He drew away from her, then reached for her again. He twined a lock of her hair through his fingers, holding it for a moment before releasing it. A single strand remained behind. With a smile, he slid it into a pocket of his trousers. "Treat my rooms as your own. Use the words dim and brighten for the lights." He left, closing the door behind him.

She wanted to run after him so she could keep him in her sight. It was only the fact that there was nothing she could do to help, that stopped her. Pacing the room, she thought about all the things she should have learned how to do instead of participating in things like gymnastics, dancing, Little Athletics and swimming. She hadn't stuck with any of them for very long. There'd been a couple of martial arts classes, but she'd spent more time giggling with her friends than paying attention. Okay, so maybe the swimming classes had been a good idea, but the rest of them not so much.

By the time Brynn returned, she'd fallen asleep in one of the armchairs. She woke as he carried her to the bed. "What time is it?" She blinked sleepily up at him.

He placed her on the bed. "Nearly morning. I didn't want to wake you, but I have to leave. I'll be back as soon as possible."

She reached for him, pulling him to her so she could kiss him. Clinging to him, she wanted to beg him to stay. At the same time she wanted to tell him to go and never come back. It wasn't safe for him here. If only she could go too. That would be crazy. Brynn had enough problems without making Elon angrier with him.

It was Brynn who drew away first. He reached out and brushed his hand across the pocket with the shell. "If anything happens, call me. And if it's urgent remember to crush the shell after you do."

She could only nod. She watched as he walked to the door, curling her hands into fists so she didn't run after him and grab hold of him so he couldn't leave. When he turned back to stare at her for a moment she had to force herself to remain still. The scent of his magic filled the air and there was a brush against her cheek. He smiled before he turned and left. By the time she lost the battle against running after him, he'd already gone. She stood by the door leading to the corridor, which she'd opened. He was nowhere in sight.

Closing the door behind her, she slowly returned to the bed. The next three to four days were going to take forever. Sleep came slowly and was broken several times by the sound of spiders scurrying through her dreams. When she gave up on sleep, she returned to the sitting room and noticed everything Brynn had left on the small table. She'd been too devastated by him leaving to notice it earlier.

There was a selection of fruit, bread, cheese, pastries, a jar of honey, biscuits, cake, juice and water. It should last her more than four days. Did he plan to be gone longer? She picked up one of the pastries. He better not be.

The day went by as slowly as she'd expected. Several times she checked Elon's rooms, but they continued to remain empty. She borrowed two of her mum's books from his shelves in the hopes of being able to distract herself with some of her favourite stories. It didn't help. All it did was remind her of how bad her situation was.

She returned the books to Elon's room on the way to the throne room. He wasn't there. Nor was Dione or any of her people. There were a few familiar faces in the throne room, but only three she could name. Eolande, Rhodri and Noah. Where was everyone? Elon better return tomorrow so she could collect on her debt.

Bored, restless and not knowing what else to do, she tried to have an early night. Instead she tossed and turned, regularly reaching for the shell as she'd done throughout the day. The next morning she ate, used the bathroom and, leaving her backpack in Brynn's rooms, went to find Elon. He was sprawled in an armchair in his sitting room, helping himself to a bowl of diced fruit topped by fresh cream, which sat on the table.

"Where have you been?" She mentally winced at the accusing tone she used, hoping he didn't take offence at it.

"Why? Did you get caught up in some sort of trouble?" He smiled before popping a piece of fruit in his mouth.

Had that been his plan? To ditch her and let her

fend for herself in the hope that she lost the bet. She shook her head. "The only obligation I still have is to you."

"Then why do you smell of another Fae's magic?"

Her heart leapt, but she forced herself to remain calm. "I've been working on trying to find a way home, once my obligation to you is over."

"Have you found one?"

She shrugged. "This is only the eighth day I've been here. I've still got plenty of time to figure it out."

Elon smiled again. "Are you counting by the days you spend here?"

His smile made her worry that she'd say something wrong and be trapped here even longer. "My obligation to you hasn't changed." She hoped that was true. She forced a smile to her own lips. "But yours has. You owe me riding lessons as well as your original obligations to me." A manual on how to deal with the Fae would have been extremely handy.

"As you said, it's only been eight days. We have plenty of time for those lessons." He dismissed her with a wave of his hand. "Attend me at dinner. Make sure you dress appropriately."

She glared at him, trying to figure out a way to demand that he teach her how to ride now.

"You may go." There was a frosty edge to his tone.

She was about to argue with him, when the solution dawned on her. "Do you honestly think it will only take me a few lessons to learn how to ride?"

"I can always teach you once you return to your own world."

She struggled to hold on to her anger. "That surprises me. I wouldn't have thought you'd want your obligation to me to last any longer than my obligation to you."

There was a hard edge to his expression. "I told you that you may go."

She guessed she'd pushed him far enough. Turning, she headed for the door. It wasn't until she opened it that he spoke again.

"Where is your ratty bag?"

She looked over her shoulder. "I found somewhere safe to keep it." She left the room, closing the door behind her before he had a chance to speak.

Chapter Fifteen

Hurrying away from Elon's rooms, Melody glanced over her shoulder to see if he would follow. Instead she saw Pirro heading in the other direction. She froze, staring after him. What was he doing around here? Had he come to visit Elon and changed his mind when he found her in the room? He disappeared around a corner and she stood there a moment longer trying to decide what to do.

Sighing, she retreated to Brynn's rooms. There was no point in following Pirro. If he noticed and came after her, she was likely to freeze. She spent the rest of the day in Brynn's rooms, bored but worried about running into any of the arachnid people. When it was close to dinnertime, she left her backpack in Brynn's sitting room and returned to Elon's. He wasn't there, but he'd left a dress for her.

She was relieved it wasn't the one covered in the

cobweb pattern. This dress was red and embroidered with gold thread that swirled over the dress in an intricate pattern. A matching drawstring bag lay beside it. She took the garment back to Brynn's rooms to change, shoving her own clothes into her backpack.

Reaching the throne room, she couldn't help looking to where Brynn would normally sit. There was another Fae in his place. A man with a trimmed beard and flowing white-blond hair that shifted around his shoulders as he turned to speak to the person beside him. As if he could feel her gaze on him, he looked in her direction. After a moment, he raised his goblet to her in a toast, smiling before he took a sip. She looked away, hurrying across the room to stand at Elon's shoulder. Elon barely glanced in her direction, focused on talking to his dinner companion.

Melody tried to pay attention to the conversations around her in case there was valuable information, but they all seemed completely uninteresting and about very little at all. Who cared which Fae were throwing parties, what the queen had worn while she'd gone riding earlier or that some Fae had lost a bet to another Fae.

When the meal ended and the tables were cleared

away, the Fae danced to the music Noah played. Melody decided he didn't look any better, but no worse either. She thought of the charm that was still in the pocket of her jeans. It seemed wrong to add it to her mum's bracelet.

Since Elon didn't dismiss her, she hovered nearby, dancing Fae brushing past her as she waited for him to tell her she could leave. He paid her no attention, dancing with partner after partner. Her boredom became annoyance and several times she had to stop herself from saying something to Elon.

A Fae grabbed her around the waist, spinning her around with the other dancers. She tried to pull away from the arms that trapped her. The Fae drew her closer, laughing as he spun her faster. The room became a blur of colour and light and fear made her heart race. Where was Elon? Was this why he hadn't dismissed her? Had he decided to make her remain in areas where she'd be fair game to the other Fae?

She wasn't about to let that happen. Deliberately stumbling, she came down hard on the Fae's foot. His grin disappeared and he staggered into another couple, his arms loosening as he turned to apologise. She pulled away from him, slipping through the crowd before he could capture her again.

The room still spun and she ran into several couples

who danced around her, mumbling apologies as she stepped away from them. Where was Elon? She had no idea where he was and the crowd pressed in around her. Fear was replaced by anger. He could have dismissed her. It wasn't like he needed her to follow him like she was his shadow. The crowd in front of her parted and the man who'd noticed her earlier came out of it. He was in front of her before she had the chance to get out of his way.

He reached for a lock of her hair. "Beautiful."

Why did the Fae all have to be so focused on her hair? Would he be offended if she pulled away from him? A couple danced away from her left and Elon took their place, drawing her hair from the man's fingers.

"She is yours?"

Melody wanted to protest against the words. No one owned her. But things didn't work that way around here. At least the room had finally stopped spinning.

Elon inclined his head. "What brings you to the castle, Reed? We haven't seen you around here for months."

"Looking for a diversion." Reed's gaze momentarily rested on Melody.

She wanted to hide behind Elon. Or run. Why did

the Fae have to find her so fascinating? There was nothing special about her.

"There are always diversions to be found at the court," Elon said.

"It looks like you've found your own." Again Reed glanced towards Melody.

Elon gave a half shrug. "An ornament. Nothing more."

Melody glared at him. It took all her effort not to argue about his indifferent comment. Why didn't he dismiss her?

Reed looked her over, his gaze travelling from head to toe and back again. "Surely there's more to her than that."

Elon gave another half shrug. "Very little." His gaze met Melody's. "She reads passably well."

"I have a book of sonnets my last protégé wrote that I'd enjoy having read to me," Reed said.

"I didn't know you had an interest in humans. When was that?"

"Centuries ago." Reed made a vague motion with his hand. "I didn't keep him long. I gave him the fruit to release our hold over him and sent him back to his own world. I believe he wrote a play based on what he saw here. I should see if I can obtain a copy and see how accurate it is."

"I'm sure I could procure a copy of it for you."

"No. Completely unnecessary. When I feel the desire to read it I'll seek out a copy for myself." Reed's gaze was drawn to Melody. "What I would like is your protégé in exchange for the favour you owe me."

"This would clear the debt I owe you if I transfer her obligation to me over to you?"

Melody barely managed not to show how shocked she was. Then she realised exactly what Elon had said. "I'm only obligated to him until the day of my eighteenth birthday in the human world on the seventh of December. Less than a year away."

"Nearly a full human year," Elon said.

"You would have offered so little to clear the debt you owe me?" Reed demanded.

Melody looked from one to the other, wishing she could leave. Speaking up looked like it was going to cause a fight, but she hadn't wanted to risk being stuck here any longer. Another thought occurred to her. "What about Elon's obligations to me? Who would they belong to if I became Reed's protégé?"

"What are they?" Reed asked.

"Almost nothing at all. Triflings," Elon said.

Reed continued to look at Melody. "What is your name?"

"Melody."

"What are his obligations?" Reed held up a hand to silence Elon when he started to speak.

Melody glanced towards Elon. With the look he gave her, she was extremely glad he couldn't harm her. Although that might change. "He said no harm would come to me from him and he'd teach me how to ride a horse."

Reed turned to Elon. "One tenth of what you owe me."

"You mock me with that offer." Elon gestured towards Melody, his gaze remaining on Reed. "Look at her. She's worth at least half."

"You told me she's little more than an ornament. I could have a sculptor create a statue equally as beautiful for a fraction of what you ask."

"Could a statue read the sonnets to you?"

Melody took a step back, wishing she could push her way through the crowd and escape to Brynn's rooms. This couldn't be happening. They were haggling over her like she was merchandise. Only fear of what they might do kept her from demanding that they stop. When they finally settled on one fourth of what Elon owed Reed, and no repercussions for the fact Elon hadn't been the one to point out the actual terms, Melody followed Reed from the throne room, dazed. The scent of cinnamon and old rainforests momentarily clung to her. She struggled to focus, not wanting to lose her way in the maze of corridors that seemed to fill the castle.

Reed stopped at a door on the way to Brynn's rooms, holding it open and gesturing for her to go inside. She stared through the doorway at the sitting room that was similar to the other two she'd been in. This one was filled with copper tones. With a glance at Reed, she hesitantly entered the room, stopping not far from the door. She watched Reed as he closed the door behind him and made his way to one of the armchairs and sat down. He gestured to one of the other empty chairs.

She remained where she was. "Why did you…" her voice trailed off as she tried to think of the right words. Want me? Buy me? Both options made her feel uncomfortable.

"Why did I what?"

She shrugged. "I don't know. Why didn't you keep the favour Elon owed you for something more important?"

"Are you saying you have no value?"

She shook her head. "No. I just can't see what value I would have to you."

"The truth."

She frowned. "I don't understand what you mean."

"You told me the truth when Elon would have cheated me. That is rare around here."

It was her own fault? Just marvellous. "Even though I'm only here for a short amount of time?"

Reed smiled. "Are you?"

The smile made a sense of uneasiness wash over her. "The terms haven't changed. I still leave on my eighteenth birthday."

"Providing you don't end up becoming obligated to anyone else before then. It's nearly impossible to avoid entanglements in the Fae Court. Both that of the light and the dark Fae."

She couldn't help thinking about Brynn at the word entanglements. "I tend to gather favours rather than owe them."

Reed chuckled. "What do you want in exchange for the favour I owe you for preventing Elon from getting more from the bargain than he deserved?"

His words surprised her. She hoped it didn't show on her face. It hadn't occurred to her that he owed her anything. "I'm guessing ending my obligation to you will be more than you're willing to offer."

"Far more than I owe you. Try again."

"What about reducing the time I owe you?"

"By how much?"

She thought of Brynn who'd hopefully be back tomorrow. Or the next day at the latest. "A fortnight to myself? When I don't need to attend you."

"I'll give you ten days."

"Fae days?"

Reed smiled. "You've learned some of our ways."

She shrugged. What could he expect with how the Fae were?

"Ten Fae days without needing to answer to me."

"Thank you."

He gestured to a bookcase that sat against the middle of one of the walls. "Fetch the book of sonnets and read them to me."

She read to him until it was late, heading for the door when she'd been dismissed for the night. She planned to stay in Brynn's room. The less time she spent around the Fae the less chance she had of becoming indebted to any of them.

Reed stopped in the doorway of his bedroom. "Where are you going?"

"My room."

"Where is it in case I should need you to attend me?"

"I know how to find my way there, but not how to tell someone else how to find it." She shrugged. "It'd be nice if there were street signs or something. Elon always told me when he wanted me to attend him. Or left me a note on his coffee table to let me know." She gestured towards the table near the armchairs.

"That will do for now. We'll have to come up with a better method. Return here when you wake in the morning." He closed the bedroom door.

She stared at it for a moment before she stepped into the corridor, wanting to leave before he changed his mind. When she reached Brynn's rooms, she put on her own clothes and left the dress over the back of one of the armchairs, having something to eat before she retired.

As she lay in the darkness, she couldn't stop thinking about Brynn and hoping he was okay. Was he and his knights on the way back? She withdrew the shell from her pocket and held it tightly in her hand as she fell asleep.

Chapter Sixteen

A pounding on the door leading to the corridor dragged her from sleep. She staggered through to the sitting room. About to open the door, she hesitated. "Who is it?"

"Open the door."

She swung it open. "Reed? How did you find me?"

He held up a strand of hair. "I found this on the floor where you'd been standing last night. Why haven't you come to my rooms like you were ordered?"

She continued to stand in the doorway, the door only half open. "You woke me."

"You wanted riding lessons. I've organised a quiet mare for you."

It took a few seconds for his words to sink in. "Give me twenty. I need to eat."

"Twenty what?"

"Minutes."

Reed nodded. "I'll meet you at the stables." He started to turn away. "Can you find your way there?"

She'd been about to tell him to wait when he'd started to leave. "No, but I can find my way to your rooms."

With a single nod, he walked away.

Melody stared after him for a moment, hoping that meant he'd wait. She closed the door and hurried across the room, needing to eat so she could have her first lesson. It didn't take her long to get ready for the day and she was at Reed's rooms in less than twenty minutes, relieved to find he'd waited for her.

Reed rose to his feet the moment she opened the door. He was leaving the room before she had a chance to come in and he strode through the corridors without speaking or even looking in her direction. Melody sent frequent glances towards him, trying to gauge his mood. By the time they stepped outside, she'd come to the conclusion that she had no idea. Reaching the stables, she ignored the white horses that were saddled and held by one of the stablehands. Her attention was drawn to the black horse that paced and threw his head up and down, snorting.

"Sorrow?" The horse trotted over to her and she

reached out to pat him on the neck. The horse shied away from her. "Where's Brynn?" She kept her voice soft, conscious of the Fae and humans who watched her.

"Have you changed your mind about lessons?" Reed asked.

She shook her head. "No, I–" She broke off abruptly when she spotted cobwebs on the saddle. Her breath caught in her throat and she tried to force herself to keep breathing. There were no spiders. Only webs. But she couldn't help think that there were places they could be hiding on the saddle. Places where a small spider could be waiting for the unwary.

"Melody?"

She couldn't drag her gaze away from the webs. They weren't very big. Something a small spider would spin.

"Melody."

Reed's sharp tone caught her attention and she glanced towards him before her gaze was once again drawn back to the webs.

"I have more important things I could be doing," Reed said.

She reached towards the horse again and this time he let her place her hand against his neck. "Good boy." She kept her voice soft, trying not to look at the webs. There were no spiders on them. At least not that she could see. No. She couldn't think that way. The spiders were long gone. They had to be.

Reed's hand dropped onto her shoulder. "Leave the horse and come have your lesson. If you aren't interested in learning you shouldn't have made an issue over it."

A stablehand joined them with nervous glances towards the horse. "Sir, could your human help us unsaddle the horse? The poor beast is too agitated to let anyone near him. He came racing in here late yesterday afternoon. Riderless."

Melody was finally able to draw her gaze away from the cobwebs. She stared at the stablehand, eyes narrowed. "Without Brynn?" She willed him to say Brynn had been riding Sorrow.

The stablehand took a step away from her. "No one rode him and we haven't seen his owner." The stablehand took another step back, glancing towards the horse. "You might want to check the other side."

"I haven't time for this." Reed gestured towards the horse.

Melody didn't even look in his direction. She stepped around to the other side of the horse. There were more cobwebs, but it was the rust coloured stains on them that drew her attention. Was that blood? Fear had her gaze travelling across the horse. It was hard to tell with the colour of Sorrow, but she was fairly certain there was dried blood on him. And she couldn't see a single wound. She stepped around the horse again, finally looking at Reed. "I want my ten days."

"Not until I've had at least that same amount of time."

She shook her head. "No. That wasn't the bargain."

"You didn't specify. It's only fair that you give me equal time first."

"No. A specific time wasn't set because I can take them whenever I choose."

"What is Brynn to you? I thought you said you owed no debts to other Fae."

She had no answer for him. "How did you track me with my hair this morning? Can you find anyone like that?" When Reed smiled, she had to force herself to stay still at the calculating look that crossed his face. "And does it need to be hair?" She thought of the shell Brynn had given her.

"What are you willing to offer?"

She wanted to say there was nothing she was willing to offer, but how could she leave Brynn with Dione? Images flashed through her mind. Brynn chained up with his sword out of reach, his fight against the arachnid knights and the spiders and cobwebs in the throne room. She couldn't bear to think Dione might have killed him already. "What were you thinking would be a fair exchange?"

"You for as long as I choose to keep you here."

"No." The word burst from her. She tried to remain calm, but it was nearly impossible. "You ask too much. All I need is for you to find where he is and let me have my ten days. I can do the rest." She had no idea how, but she'd figure that out once she knew where he was.

"Our horses don't leave us unless we're dead or send them away." Reed gestured towards Sorrow. "If Brynn is still alive, the area you want me to take you to will be full of danger for anyone allied with him."

"I don't need you to get close as long as you can show me the location."

"What if I need to get close to be able to show you the location?"

She had no answer for him. "Then give me my ten days and I'll find him on my own."

"Come with me." Reed didn't wait for her, but strode to a secluded area of the stableyard.

Not wanting to leave Sorrow by himself she took hold of his reins and led him over to Reed. The horse shied from every sound and movement. What had happened to him and Brynn?

"I have plans for you over the next few days." Reed kept his voice low.

"What sort of plans?" She ran her hand along Sorrow's neck, wishing he could tell her what had happened.

"I need you to retrieve something for me."

Melody shook her head. "That wasn't the deal. I'm ornamental only. Elon told you that."

"An ornament who can read. It will make the perfect excuse if you should be caught."

She continued to shake her head. "That wasn't the bargain."

"You're obligated to obey me."

"I owe you no more than I owed Elon." At least she hoped not. Actually, she owed him even less since she had ten days of freedom. "Let me go for ten days and I'll try and retrieve whatever it is that you want when I get back."

"You might not return." Reed's gaze was drawn to Sorrow. "It's almost a certainty you won't return."

She wanted to disagree with him, but he probably had more time for arguing than she did. "What did you want retrieved?" Reed stared at her for nearly a minute. She wanted to tell him to hurry up and speak. Brynn was in danger and Reed was wasting her time.

"Eolande has a large pink diamond that is heart shaped. There are other Fae that have similar ones, but none as large or as flawless as hers." He paused, continuing to hold her gaze. "Until recently."

She had no idea what that had to do with her. "And?"

"What exactly are you asking?"

His words made her think of Brynn and her grip tightened on the reins. "Everything."

Reed frowned. "We haven't time for me to tell you everything and nor would I wish to do so."

"Everything to do with what you expect from me."

"Has no one ever taught you how to ask questions?"

She smiled faintly. "Elon wasn't kidding when he said I'm only good at being an ornament."

"Then how do you think you're going to rescue Brynn, if he is still alive?"

"By looking pretty?" At the surprise that flashed across Reed's face, she nearly laughed. Maybe Fae didn't understand sarcasm. Worry for Brynn kept even a smile from forming. "What do you want me to do?"

"I need the diamond necklace."

"The queen's?"

"Of course not." Reed looked horrified. "I need you to retrieve Seren's diamond."

Melody guessed that must be the woman who had a diamond bigger than the queen's. "You should have made it part of the bargain. As Elon said, I'm only an ornament."

"As my protégé I would expect you to follow orders."

She shrugged. "That wasn't spelled out in the bargain either."

Reed's jaw tightened. "Are you telling me you refuse to do this small task?"

"Not exactly. What happens if I'm caught retrieving the necklace?"

"Seren will have you killed. The plan is not to be caught."

"Well, you see that's where the problem is. I only have one talent and that is being a passable reader. You want me to do something way beyond my abilities and you aren't willing to offer something decent in return."

"What do you want?"

She was torn between wanting his help to rescue Brynn and ending her obligations to him. She thought of Noah and the favour he owed her. Maybe she could solve both her problems. "All obligations to you finished."

Reed laughed. A humourless, mocking sound. "What I've asked of you isn't even worth a tenth of what you owe me."

His comment reminded her of the negotiations between him and Elon last night. Maybe a tenth was his favourite starting bid. "How about all my obligations to you are ended and I never mention to anyone about your request?"

"You wouldn't be so stupid as to tell others about my affairs."

The threat in his tone made her want to agree to anything he said. His green eyes glittered and his body was tensed, ready to attack. She couldn't give in. There was very little she had to bargain with. "As long as I'm your protégé, your secret is safe. A human year is such a small amount of time."

"The same applies to me. You are only safe from me harming you for as long as our bargain lasts. Do you think I would let you go so you could tell other Fae my business?"

She tried to ignore the fear that coursed through her at his words. Dipping her fingers into her pocket she brushed the tips against the shell. "I have others who owe me favours and would make certain I survived."

"Who? Brynn?" Reed nodded towards Sorrow. "It appears one of your allies is in no position to help you."

"He isn't the only one who owes me a favour." She wasn't crazy enough to give him names. "Why does the queen want you to retrieve the diamond? Why doesn't she make Seren give it to her?"

Chapter Seventeen

"I'm beginning to think Elon wasn't exaggerating about your stupidity," Reed said.

Melody took a deep breath and shrugged carelessly, forcing a smile to her lips, assuming her guess had been incorrect. "Aren't favours meant to be equal? You're asking me to do something I'm not obligated to do and that's far beyond my expertise." At least she guessed it was. "Why should I risk death for you without proper compensation?"

"It's a simple enough task that you shouldn't even come close to risking death while completing it."

"Maybe for you, but humans aren't as capable as Fae. Why don't you retrieve the diamond?"

"Because there's no plausible reason for me to be in Seren's rooms."

This was taking far too long. How much time did

Brynn have? "You've suddenly fallen madly in love with her?"

He shook his head. "We were lovers decades ago. Things didn't end well."

"Then why would you send me to read sonnets to her?"

"I always send her a gift to celebrate the day she was born. That's next week."

She certainly wasn't waiting around that long. "I'll visit her today and I'll never tell anyone you asked me to steal her diamond and I'll try and get the diamond as long as my obligation to you is finished."

"That isn't acceptable. I'll take a quarter of the time off for you and neither of us will be obligated to the other for anything more. Nor will you tell anyone what I asked you to do."

"You have to be kidding me."

"Keep your voice down." Reed glanced towards the human that still held the horses for him and a second human who brought a saddled horse out to a Fae.

"What can you expect? You're trying to rip me off."

"I'm trying to do what?"

"You know, get the better part of the bargain in a major way."

"I think you're the one who's trying to do that."

There had to be a way to get out of being obligated to him. Surely she could think of something. But she couldn't.

"Well? Do you accept the terms?" Reed asked.

"Not as they are. I–" She glanced away as an idea occurred to her. "If I'm caught I'll make sure you aren't suspected so you can find someone else to steal the diamond for you."

"Retrieve."

She shrugged. "Fine, retrieve the diamond."

"How do you think you can manage that? If the queen demands a name, you'll be forced to tell her as her magic is far more powerful than mine."

"If I can get the diamond for you without anyone finding out you were the one who sent me to retrieve it, then my obligation to you is complete. If I fail and survive being caught and manage not to name you, then my obligation to you is halved and I can use my ten days whenever I want."

Reed examined her silently. He nodded once before holding out his hand. "It's a deal."

When she took his hand, the scent of cinnamon washed over her. "Where's Seren's room?"

"Meet me back at my room in half an hour. You'll

need something to help you in case anything is locked."

"I don't know my way around here."

Reed sighed heavily. "I'll show you to my room, then I'll return with a crystal imbued with a spell that will enable you to unlock things. Except those that are locked with highly complex spells."

"I need to unsaddle the horse first." Sorrow had finally started to calm down.

"Make it quick."

She led Sorrow into the stable, taking him to the stall she'd last seen him in. A stablehand took the saddle and bridle from her and when she was alone with the horse, she moved close to whisper to him. "I will find him, Sorrow. I wish you could tell me what happened." She withdrew the shell from her pocket and pressed it against her lips. "Brynn." There was no answer. She didn't know what she'd expected.

The horse nickered softly, resting his head on her shoulder for a moment.

"Did he send you away or did something happen to make you leave him?"

Sorrow snorted, shaking his head.

She smiled slightly. "I could almost believe you were trying to talk to me." She patted him one last time before she left the stable, striding towards Reed.

He strode off before she reached him and she followed, wondering how long the spell lasted on the crystal he was going to give her for using on locks. Was it permanent? Or did it only have a set amount of uses? When they reached Reed's rooms, she spoke when he would have immediately left. "How many things can I unlock with the crystal?"

"At least a dozen, depending on how well locked they are."

"Will that be enough?"

"I should think so." He turned and left the room, closing the door behind him.

She dropped into an armchair to wait for him, then decided she should probably choose a book of poetry to read to Seren. Not the sonnets in case it was known that they belong to Reed. The poetry would still make a good excuse if she was discovered, she just needed to give another reason, other than Reed, for why she was there to read the poems. Maybe the thought of a secret admirer would intrigue Seren.

When Reed returned, she was slumped in one of the armchairs, reading the poems. She rose to her feet, taking the clear crystal he held out to her. Tucking it into a different pocket to the shell, she pushed thoughts of Brynn away, straightening her shoulders.

She couldn't think of him if she wanted to get through this task. "Where is her room?"

"Follow me. When I look at you that will mean her room is on our right. Afterwards, take a different direction to me and come back to her room once a few minutes have passed."

Melody nodded and followed Reed from the room, making sure she took note of the different corridors they travelled through. When Reed glanced behind him, meeting her gaze, she looked at the door on her right. Why couldn't they have street signs and numbers to make it easier to find everything?

She continued to follow Reed until she found a corridor to turn into. It wasn't far from Brynn's rooms and she decided to change into one of her dresses. They were probably more suitable than her jeans for reading romantic poems from an imaginary secret admirer.

She wore the red dress that was embroidered with gold thread, using the matching drawstring bag so she could put the shell and crystal in it. Since she wasn't about to wear the boots with the web pattern, even if Elon would let her collect them from his room, she left her sneakers on. Her stomach did a slow back flip and she pressed her hand against it, wishing she had a better idea of the way things worked around here. But she didn't and Brynn needed help. She'd just have to figure it out as she went along.

When she reached Seren's room, she knocked on the door and waited for an answer. There was none. She tried the handle and was surprised when it swung open. Unlike the other rooms she'd been in, Seren only had a single room. A large bed was in the centre of the far wall, there were two armchairs clustered in one corner and a dressing table and wardrobe were on the wall opposite them. The room was decorated in silver and pink.

Closing the door behind her, she searched the room. Spread across the duchess and in the numerous containers decorating its surface she found a heap of jewellery with pink stones, but not a single one was heart shaped. Catching sight of the frantic look in her eyes in the mirror above the duchess, she tried to remain calm. It didn't help. Turning away she took several hesitant steps and stood in the middle of the room, wondering what to do. The bargain hadn't covered being unable to find the necklace. Why hadn't she at least bargained for some time off the obligation for attempting but failing to find it?

The door swung open and a tall, slim, fair-haired woman entered the room, her hair almost silvery in its paleness. Melody's gaze was drawn to the necklace she wore. A large pink heart shaped stone with two small white hearts on either side. She guessed this was Seren.

"Who are you and what are you doing here?"

Melody hastily held up the book of poetry. "I was waiting for you to return so I could read this to you." She forced a smile to her lips, trying to relax even though she wanted to grab the necklace that hung at the woman's neck and run.

"Who sent you?"

Melody struggled to keep her smile in place, ignoring the suspicion filling Seren's voice. "A secret admirer."

Seren entered the room properly, closing the door. "Aren't you Elon's pet?"

She shook her head. "No, but even when I was his pet I did favours for others."

"Why would you do favours for someone who isn't your master?"

"Only the weak have no allies." It was a line from one of her mum's books.

Seren laughed. A sound like water cascading over rocks. "You've been Elon's pet far too long."

Melody tried to focus on the conversation instead of trying to figure out how anyone could laugh like that. Was it magic? Or just something some of the Fae were capable of? "Oh, I don't know. I think any time as his pet is far too long."

Seren laughed again. "You're amusing." She crossed the space between them, reaching out to lift a lock of Melody's hair and run it through her fingers. "I can see your appeal. But I'm afraid you're wasting your time. I need to get ready to go riding with the court."

Melody continued to look into Seren's pale blue eyes. She wasn't game to look anywhere else for fear she'd focus on the necklace. "I'll sit in one of the armchairs and read to you while you get ready to go riding. Surely you're interested in hearing what poems your secret admirer finds suitable for you."

Seren looked her up and down a few times before she nodded and gestured towards the corner with the armchairs. "You may read, but if I find your voice annoying you may tell my secret admirer they need to try better next time."

Melody nodded and headed to the armchair, relieved she could finally stop smiling. She thought of the poems she'd read earlier, recalling one that seemed appropriate. It spoke about moonlight on water and compared it to a woman's hair. Hopefully Seren would take it as a compliment. Sitting in the chair, she turned to the appropriate page and began to read. As she read, she sent frequent glances towards Seren, but the Fae didn't remove her necklace. She finished that poem and went on to another, this one talking about a woman someone loved from afar because he felt he was too insignificant for her to notice. Knowing the arrogance of most Fae, Melody was pretty certain Seren would enjoy this one.

Seren finished changing into a rose pink riding habit edged with silver and stood staring at herself in the mirror on the wall above the duchess. Melody was relieved she didn't stumble when Seren ran her fingers over the pink diamond. She kept reading, going on to the next poem, speaking the words without paying attention to them as she shot more frequent glances towards Seren.

When Seren undid the clasp of the necklace and dropped it into a container on the duchess, Melody nearly stopped breathing. She forced herself to continue to read, reaching the end of the poem and rising to her feet. She kept her gaze on Seren, who now faced her, and smiled. "I hope you enjoyed those poems."

"The first two I could understand my admirer choosing, but why would they choose the last one?"

Melody glanced at the book she still held,

wondering what she'd read. She shrugged. "I'm only the messenger."

"Who'd want to be compared to a tale of two lovers who died in each other's arms?"

Melody's heart sank. That had obviously not been a good choice. She struggled to keep her smile in place. "Maybe your admirer is telling you they'll love you forever, even beyond death."

Seren continued to look at her a moment longer before she nodded, her frown clearing. "Well of course they would." She gestured towards the door. "You may go now."

"Are there any messages you'd like me to pass along?"

Seren let the silence draw out before she spoke. "No." She smiled, a sharp, cat-like smile. One about to toy with its prey.

Melody nodded and hurried to the door, not wanting to be the prey.

"If you have nothing else you must do this evening after the feast, you may attend me and read until I fall asleep."

Melody looked over her shoulder, a hand resting on the doorknob. No way did she want to spend any more time with Seren than necessary. "I'm sorry. I'm afraid my time isn't my own this evening. If I ever find myself with some free time of an evening when you're ready to retire, I'll remember your request." When Seren gave her a dismissive nod, she stepped into the corridor, closing the door behind her.

Chapter Eighteen

Melody paused outside the door, wondering what she could do. It wasn't like she could wait around until Seren left. That'd be too obvious. She walked slowly down the corridor, glancing at the closed doors she passed. She couldn't stop thinking about the necklace Seren had dropped in the trinket box. Glancing over her shoulder, she saw the corridor was still empty. Reaching an intersection, she stepped into it and waited, peering around the edge towards Seren's door. Her heart jumped when Seren stepped into the corridor and headed in her direction. She had no idea what to do. Running wasn't an option. Not if she wanted to help Brynn. Staring at her feet, her attention was caught by the laces of her sneakers. Grinning, she placed the book on the floor, crouching to retie her laces. Keeping her head lowered she kept an eye on the corridor, waiting for

Seren to walk past before she stood up and peered around the corner.

As soon as Seren was out of sight she hurried back to the room, relieved to find the door unlocked. Glancing around the room she walked straight to the duchess, half expecting someone would jump out of hiding and demand what she was doing. Picking up the trinket box, she tried to open the lid and found it was locked. Returning it to the duchess she withdrew the crystal and pressed it against the latch. Nothing happened. Dropping the crystal in the drawstring bag, she tried to open the little box again. It continued to remain locked.

She glanced around the room, not sure what to do. In the end, she crammed the box into the drawstring bag, unable to fully close it. As long as no one looked at it closely they shouldn't notice the box. She raced across the room and opened the door a crack to peer into the corridor. It was empty and she slipped out, softly closing the door. Her heart continued to race as she walked away from Seren's room and she kept expecting someone to demand what she was doing. She didn't stop peering over her shoulder every few seconds until she'd reached Reed's room and slipped inside.

He rose from the armchair he'd been sitting in. "Did you manage to retrieve it?"

She tugged the box from the drawstring bag and held it out to him. "I couldn't get it unlocked."

Taking the box, he pressed his hand against the lock. The smell of cinnamon filled the room and the lid of the box popped open. Reed drew the necklace out, smiling. "She doesn't suspect anything?"

Melody shook her head and told him about the excuse she'd used and returning to the room after Seren had left. "She even asked me to read her to sleep tonight."

"What did you tell her?"

Melody struggled not to smile. She didn't want him to think it had been too easy. "It took me a bit to convince her my time wasn't my own tonight."

Reed returned the necklace to the box and closed it. "You may go. Our debt to each other is ended other than yours to never speak of this."

The smell of cinnamon washed over her again and she nodded, not bothering to say anything before slipping out of the room and returning to Brynn's.

She changed into her jeans and t-shirt before having something to eat and packing items into her backpack she thought she might need for the journey. Thinking of all the blood on the horse, she added a change of clothes for Brynn, leaving most of hers behind. Food was more important as she didn't know how long it would take.

Leaving the backpack in the room, she went looking for Noah. It took far longer than she would have liked, but she eventually found him in the walled garden. He was practising. She waited for him to finish his tune before she spoke. "I need to find a Fae who can enchant something so I can find someone."

"None of the Fae I know has that ability."

"What if I request it as my favour from you?"

"It'd take me at least a week to find someone. This isn't an ability every Fae has and those who can don't always let others know they're capable of tracing people. You need powerful magic to be able to do it."

She wanted to argue against his words. "Surely you know someone."

Noah gave a half shrug. "Well I actually know two people, but there's no way I'd ask the king or queen to do something like that. No one would ask it of them."

She stared at him trying to figure out what to do. The last thing she wanted was to return to Reed and become indebted to him again. She felt like screaming in frustration. "You know absolutely no one?" She wanted to beg him to tell her he could help. Reed wasn't an option she wanted to take.

"Is it urgent? I can ask around. Who are you trying to find?"

"Never mind." She strode from the gardens, heading for Reed's rooms. They were empty. She sat in an armchair and tapped her fingers on her leg while she waited, eventually pacing the room. Reed still didn't return. Hours passed and she became hungry, but didn't dare leave the room for fear she'd miss him. Several times she considered checking the throne room, thinking he might be at dinner. But what if she missed him along the way? When he did return, she was once again slumped in an armchair and jumped to her feet the moment he entered.

He stepped only far enough into the room to close the door behind him. "Did I not say our dealings were over?"

"I need help finding Brynn."

Reed smirked. "Really?"

She felt like groaning. He wasn't going to play nice. "Yes."

"Double the time you owed me previously. No days of freedom."

She shook her head. "I can get it cheaper than that.

I just thought you'd be more reasonable considering all I've done for you."

Reed stepped to the side and gestured towards the door. "Go ahead then."

"Let's forget about the haggling and I'll give you a realistic deal. A quarter of the time."

He laughed at her. "Do you take me for a fool? You wouldn't have returned if you had any other choice. Wasn't the horse able to tell you much?"

She struggled to keep her expression neutral. From all she knew after her dealings with Reed, he didn't do sarcasm. She needed to talk to Noah again. "Is that your answer? Double? Because I'm not willing to accept such a ridiculous offer." How was she meant to find Noah at this time of night?

"The same time as before then."

Melody slowly shook her head. "No. You heard my offer. I'll come back in the morning. Give you some time to think about a more realistic offer." She stepped past him, reaching for the door.

"Who else are you negotiating with?"

Melody looked over her shoulder, smiling. "Do you take me for a fool?" She stepped out the door and strode towards the walled garden. It was empty. She hadn't thought Noah would be there, but it had been worth a try. He also wasn't in the throne room or the numerous empty corridors she wandered along.

She returned to Brynn's room tired, hungry, worried and having no clue what she should do next. Sitting in an armchair, she had a snack while she tried to think of her options. Once she'd finished eating, she fell asleep while trying to come up with a plan. It was early morning when she woke and she raced to the door, panicked at how much time had passed since Brynn had gone missing. She was halfway along the corridor before she calmed down enough to return to Brynn's room and get ready for the morning, including having a hurried breakfast. She slipped on her backpack before she left the room.

The first place she checked for Noah was the walled garden. She heard him before she saw him, his music filling the garden. This time she didn't wait for him to finish. "Who can talk to horses and understand them?"

He stopped playing, glaring at her. "Any of the Fae that run the stables. A few of the humans who've gained Fae magic." He shrugged. "Others. It isn't an overly rare talent."

"Can you?"

"My talent lies with music." He sounded offended.

Melody tried not to sigh. She didn't have time for

this. "I need you to negotiate for someone to question a horse for me." That wasn't a comment she'd ever thought to make. It made her sound insane.

"What do you have to bargain with?"

"Your favour."

"No."

"Are you telling me you refuse to repay me for the help I gave you?"

"I owe you, not someone else."

"And I want you to use the favour you owe me to get answers from a horse I need to question." It sounded just as insane as before.

"Whose horse?"

"Brynn's." When Noah stumbled backwards, his skin paling, she wanted to demand what he knew. "When I have the answers, your debt to me is paid."

"Are you trying to get me killed? I don't want anything to do with him."

Her hands tightened into fists. "You will repay the favour you owe me or I might happen to mention how you refused to repay all I did for you and exactly what it was I did." Her heart sank at the anger she saw in his eyes. He would retaliate. Hopefully she'd be back in the human world before he had the chance.

With a curt nod, Noah strode towards the corridor, still holding onto his violin and bow. He walked silently through the castle, not speaking until he reached the stables. He barely glanced at her. "Wait here."

She watched as he disappeared inside the stables and wondered if she shouldn't have followed him to make sure he didn't double cross her. He took long enough that she was about to go and find him when he came out, followed by a human. The man was taller than Noah and looked to be in his thirties, but that didn't mean much in this realm. He had olive skin, a narrow frame that was nearly as slim as the light Fae and green eyes that seemed unnaturally pale compared to his dark brown hair.

Noah gestured to the man who stood beside him. "This is Carden. He's willing to ask the horse six questions."

Carden nodded in greeting.

Melody wanted to protest that she might need more than six questions. As had been pointed out to her several times, she wasn't very good at asking them. Instead, she smiled in greeting, trying not to let the urgency and desperation she felt show.

"We are done." Noah held her gaze, still looking angry.

Melody nodded. "Yes."

Noah didn't bother saying goodbye, striding back

to the castle with his violin in one hand and the bow in the other.

"When do you want to ask the questions?"

She faced Carden. "Now." She followed him inside the stable and to Sorrow's stall. The horse seemed less agitated than it had been yesterday.

"What do you want me to ask him?"

"What happened?"

"You need to be more specific than that."

She nearly growled. "What happened to Brynn?"

Carden reached for Sorrow who initially shied away. He placed his palm against the horse's forehead and murmured softly.

Melody struggled to hear what he said, but he spoke too quietly. Sorrow snorted then nickered softly. How could Carden make sense of those sounds? Or was there some other way he communicated?

Carden looked towards her, keeping his hand on Sorrow's forehead. "Brynn was attacked by ten arachnid knights."

"Is he alive?"

Carden nodded. "He was when Sorrow last saw him."

"Where did they take him?"

"Towards Dione's holdings."

"How can I find him? I don't know where her holdings are."

"He says he can take you there."

She had two questions left. Maybe she was getting better at asking them. "I'll leave the rest of the questions for another day."

Carden nodded and dropped his hand, stepping away from the horse. "Will that be all?"

"I need Sorrow saddled."

"I'll saddle him in exchange for both the questions."

"One question."

Carden nodded and walked away.

She guessed that meant she still had one question left. Not that she knew what to do with it. But who knew when something like that would come in handy when it came to dealing with the Fae. Or the humans in this realm.

Chapter Nineteen

It didn't take Carden long to saddle Sorrow and Melody took the reins he held out. "Thank you."

He nodded and helped her onto the horse before walking off without another word.

She stared after him, grabbing at Sorrow's mane when he shifted impatiently. When he remained still, she let go of his mane and tried to figure out how to hold the reins. Nothing felt right. She sighed. "Okay. Let's go, but take it easy. I don't know how to ride." She hoped he understood her.

They came out of the stable and she nearly fell off the horse when she heard what two of the stablehands were talking about. Sorrow came to a stop and she tried to seat herself in a more secure position as she listened.

"Eolande is livid. She'd expected Seren to return the

diamond to her in fifty years, once the bargain was ended."

"Does anyone know what happened?"

"Seren keeps trying to say it was stolen."

The second stablehand snorted. "She's forever losing things. Careless, that's what she is."

Melody wanted to tell Sorrow to stop, but she didn't want the stablehands to realise she was interested in their conversation. What was Reed planning? No wonder he didn't want anyone to know he'd stolen the diamond. It was actually the queen's. Or at least it would be again in fifty years. She was tempted to check over her shoulder to see what the stablehands were doing, but she'd probably fall off. A pity she'd never managed to get those riding lessons.

She was still thinking the same thing when the sun set and Sorrow continued to take her through a forest. Her body ached and the ride seemed far more jarring than when she'd ridden behind Brynn. She had no idea what she was doing wrong. Eventually Sorrow came to a stop at the edge of a forest and she wondered if she should hop off him. She doubted she'd be able to get back on without help. She hadn't stopped to eat and drink, and had been worried she'd fall off if she attempted to do either on horseback.

Moonlight filtered through the trees showing little more than dark shapes. "What now?"

Sorrow tossed his head.

"I have no idea what that's supposed to mean." When he continued to remain there, she dismounted, landing on her backside. How did everyone manage to make it look so easy? She sent the horse a narrowed eyed look as she dusted off the seat of her jeans. "Couldn't you have knelt like a camel or something?"

Sorrow snorted, turning his head towards her.

"Well it would have helped." Since she was off the horse, she had a long drink from one of her water bottles.

Sorrow snorted again.

"I know." He didn't need to keep hurrying her. She knew she didn't have time to waste, but letting herself dehydrate wasn't going to help either. Anyway, he couldn't complain since he'd stopped to drink from a stream earlier.

Returning the bottle to the backpack she stepped past him, peering through the trees to the open meadow at the forest's edge. Towering over the landscape was a castle silhouetted by moonlight. Towers shot into the sky from random points throughout the castle, cobwebs strung between them.

Melody reached for the tree beside her and clung

to the rough bark. "He's in there?" Her words were a whisper.

Sorrow came forward to blow against her cheek, nuzzling her.

It didn't help. She wanted to clamber on his back and race as far from here as possible. She slipped her fingers into her pocket and brushed against the shell. How was she going to find Brynn in a castle? He could be anywhere. "What now? How do you expect me to find him?" She stumbled forward when Sorrow nudged her shoulder blade. Standing away from the trees made her feel exposed. She took a step back. "Okay. Fine. I take it I need to go in there. But I'll do it after I've had something to eat."

She wasn't putting the moment off. She knew how urgent it was to go after Brynn. Dione wanted him dead. Probably after she'd made him suffer. It made sense to have something to eat before she went inside. Who knew when she'd have the chance again? She was starving and would have to leave her backpack behind. It was too bulky to take into a place she'd need to sneak through.

After she'd eaten and drank some more of the water, she tied her backpack onto the saddle with the straps that she unbuckled. She stared at Sorrow, wishing she could see him better, then was immediately glad for the darkness that hid them. "You'll wait for me, won't you?" When Sorrow nickered, she felt slightly relieved. "I'll take that as a yes." She faced the clearing, taking a deep breath and trying not to look at the webs. She could do this.

She sighed heavily. Who was she kidding? She slipped her fingers inside her pocket to brush them against the shell. She'd probably freeze at the first sight of a cobweb, but she couldn't leave Brynn in there. So much for no entanglements.

The way seemed clear so she ran across the open meadow towards the castle. When she reached the rock wall of the castle that towered above her, she realised Sorrow had brought her to the rear of the building. Keeping close to the castle, she crept through the shadows until she found a door. Turning the handle she found it unlocked. She thought of the crystal that was still in her pocket, wondering if it would have been able to open the door if it had been locked. She stood there, trying to make herself open it enough to enter. The thought of a castle filled with arachnid people made her freeze. She tried to think of something else. Standing by the stream wrapped in Brynn's arms came to mind. She couldn't desert him.

She forced herself to step inside. Lights glowing softly in the ceiling showed her the room was empty.

Several doors led off the spacious room and a set of narrow stairs went to the upper levels. She had no idea where to go. Maybe she should have given into Reed's demands. She really hoped she didn't need to return to Eolande's castle to ask for his help. He'd probably offer her worse terms since she hadn't returned in the morning like she'd said she would. It would also mean leaving Brynn here longer. She couldn't do that. She had no idea how long he'd been here already.

Picking the door to her left, for no other reason than it was the closest, she crept down a corridor. Within minutes she was lost. Wandering around the ground floor of the castle with no idea of where to go had been a terrible idea. Hearing the sounds of footsteps, she slipped into a room, leaving the door slightly ajar. Two arachnids walked past the door and she stopped breathing, freezing in place. Light-headedness had her drawing in a deep breath and she forced herself to leave the room, trying to point out that the arachnids were long out of sight. But who knew when the next ones would come along. It was bad enough that she couldn't bring herself to look into the corners of the ceiling where she'd noticed frequent empty cobwebs. Remaining cowering in a room waiting to be found was ridiculous.

Her steps were slow and hesitant as she stayed close to one of the walls. She'd known Dione and her people lived here, but it wasn't until she'd actually seen them that the fact had sunk in properly. Each step was an effort and she had to force herself not to run. Even if she did run, she had nowhere to go. No way to get home. She doubted Sorrow would take her anywhere without Brynn.

She eventually came to another room with a set of stairs. This one led both upwards and downwards. She stared into the darkness. It seemed like the perfect place to keep an enemy. It also seemed like the perfect place for spiders to live. A shudder went through her as she took half a step towards the darkness.

Nearly a minute passed before she could bring herself to move and it was only the sound of footsteps coming towards her that had her stumbling down the stairs and hiding in the shadows underneath them. The footsteps went up the staircase and she sagged against the far wall, smothering a scream when she brushed against a cobweb.

Backing away, she wished for a light, while frantically brushing her hands over where the web had touched her. There was a dim glow in the ceiling further along the corridor and, continuing to brush the feeling of the web from her skin, she hurried towards it. Stopping beneath the soft lighting, she stared at where she could still feel the cobweb even though there was none on her. She was relieved to see there were also no spiders. Her shoulders slumped. She couldn't do this.

Turning, she looked at the stairs that were nearly indistinct in the almost darkness, a spill of light showing the top couple. She wanted to run up them and race outside. Maybe she could convince Sorrow to take her away from here. She could tell him she needed help to rescue Brynn. Sighing, she slowly shook her head. She couldn't bring herself to lie to him and she was pretty certain he wasn't about to go anywhere until Brynn could go too. She looked over her shoulder. Surely she was more capable than a horse. Although he was a Fae horse and they were obviously far different to human ones.

She faced the direction she needed to search, straightening her shoulders. No matter what she told herself, she was unable to take more than a single step. Calling herself an idiot, amongst other names, didn't bring her any closer to moving forward.

When she remembered that standing around would give the arachnids the chance to discover her, she almost ran along the corridor. She peered into rooms, opening up the doors that she passed. At one room she stood with mouth open as she stared at what appeared to be large spider eggs. Trembling she finally managed to close the door and back away from it, her breath coming too fast.

Her gaze was drawn to the stairs. She took a step in their direction before halting her retreat. She couldn't leave until she'd searched the entire place. Brynn had to be somewhere in the castle. Not that she knew how to find her way out. She was completely lost. Forcing reluctant limbs to obey her, she continued along the corridor. Three doors later she again stood frozen in a doorway. She stared at a web at the far side of the room, Brynn trapped in the middle of it and wrapped tightly in spider silk. Several soft lights shone down from the ceiling, clearly showing her the entire room. She remained in the doorway, trying to force herself forward. They were alone in the room, not even an ordinary spider with them. She had to do something before an arachnid found her.

He groaned and she hurried forward, reaching for him. She stopped, unable to bring herself to touch the web. She couldn't draw her gaze from the spider silk that was tightly wrapped around his body. Her breath was shallow and her heart raced as she continued to stand there frozen.

"Go."

Her gaze flickered to his face before returning instantly to his cocooned body.

"Melody, go."

She shook her head, still unable to look elsewhere.

"You're wasting your time. It's too late."

She finally managed to look at his face. There was a pale, bloodless look to his skin and some of his veins in his neck appeared black and prominent. "What did they do?" She could only manage a whisper.

"Poison."

Fear struck her and she swayed on the spot, her hand pressing against her mouth to hold back the protests she wanted to make. They had to get out of here. Somehow.

"Take my sword and go. It's by the door." His words were laboured.

Chapter Twenty

Turning, Melody spotted the sword and darted across the room to pick it up, drawing it from the scabbard. The weight of the weapon dragged at her arm, but she felt safer holding it.

"Melody, please. My home is too far from here and I have no allies at the light Fae Court. I'll be dead within a day. Two at the most. Go before they find you too."

She shook her head, forcing herself to return to him. "What could allies do?" She pressed the sword against the web and several strands snapped.

"Draw the poison from my body. Help me heal. I'm too weak to do it myself."

She sliced through several more strands. His body sagged to one side. "Can anyone do it?"

"If they're powerful enough."

"What about Eolande? She must like you since she

wouldn't let Dione kill you." When his body dropped to the ground, she winced.

"She likes my father and wouldn't do anything directly against him. Nor would she like to upset my relatives from the dark Fae Court. But even she wouldn't use so much energy to help me."

She slipped the tip of the blade into the top of the spider cocoon, trying not to think about the creatures who'd made it. Would Reed be powerful enough? It was no point wondering about Elon. He was friends with Dione. "Sorrow is waiting for you. He brought me here."

"I'm sorry. When I sent him to you I didn't think you'd come after me. I thought you'd let my knights know I needed help. Didn't Sorrow tell you?"

She was halfway through cutting the cocoon away. "No." Obviously she wasn't as good at asking questions as she'd thought. When he didn't speak, she said, "Keep talking. Distract me." As long as she didn't think too much or look too closely she could manage this. She hoped.

"How did you get time away from Elon?"

"I'm no longer his protégé." That sounded far better than pet.

"What happened?"

She cut through the last of the spider silk. "Reed."

"You're Reed's protégé?"

She slid the sword into the scabbard before she helped him to his feet, worried by how difficult he found it to stand. "Not anymore."

"How long have I been gone?"

His words surprised a laugh from her. "Not very long." They reached the door and she wanted to beg him to move faster. His stumbling gait terrified her. As did the dark, prominent veins that crisscrossed his arms and chest. She had no idea if his legs were the same since he wore trousers.

"Tell me everything that happened while I was gone."

They stepped into the corridor. It was empty. "The first day you were gone I mostly spent in your room. The next day I ended up as Reed's protégé. The following day, which was yesterday, I found Sorrow and stopped being Reed's protégé. I didn't realise some people could talk to horses until today."

"How did you stop being Reed's protégé?"

They reached the bottom of the steps and she sighed as she looked up the seemingly endless staircase. "By doing him a favour. You can stop talking now. Save your energy to get out of this place."

"What favour?"

"One I can't talk about." She moved forward, her arm remaining around his waist while she carried his sword in her other hand. She staggered as he leaned heavily on her to take the first step. It was going to be a long process.

When they reached the next floor, Brynn leaned against the wall, breathing heavily. "You can't stay here with me. You'll end up getting caught. Go. I'll work on getting out of here once I take a rest."

She eyed him. "Isn't it meant to be impossible for you lot to lie?" She thought of how Reed had told her Seren's necklace was better than the queen's. Did the queen own a second pink diamond necklace? It wouldn't surprise her.

"I didn't lie." He smiled slightly. "You're the one with a tendency to do that."

"Come on, Brynn. Just a little further."

He pushed away from the wall and leaned against her again. "If we're discovered, you run and take my sword with you. Present it to Sorrow and tell him he and the sword are now yours."

His words made pain and fear shoot through her. It wasn't going to happen. "Shut up and keep moving."

"Promise me you won't do anything stupid."

"I'm not stupid. As if I'm about to make any promises to you after the last one." Maybe she was stupid. She had to be, at least slightly, to have entered Dione's castle. "Where is everyone who lives here? I've hardly seen anyone."

"Apart from a handful of guards, they're probably asleep. Or out hunting."

Melody shuddered. She didn't want to think about them out hunting. Although having the castle filled with sleeping arachnids didn't sound much better. Before she could comment, she heard footsteps. The closest door was the one they'd just passed and she helped Brynn back to it, closing the door behind them.

He staggered to a nearby armchair, dropping heavily onto it. Closing his eyes, he tilted his head back. The black veins on his neck appeared worse in the dim light from the ceiling. She turned away, unable to look at him any longer. The thought of poison travelling through his veins made her feel ill. Even more so when she thought about it being spider poison. Not having any idea how late it was, she crossed the room to draw back a heavy curtain and peer outside. There was a faint hint of grey in the sky. Sunrise wasn't too far away. They had to get away before then or they might be spotted trying to cross the meadow. And the arachnids were probably starting to wake up for the day. She had no idea how they could get out of a castle full of arachnids wandering about.

Staring out the window, she looked at the small drop to the ground. It wasn't far. They could slip out the window and into the forest without the arachnids knowing. She tried to open the window. It wouldn't budge. Her heart raced and she began to think she'd be trapped in here forever. The crystal came to mind and she took several deep breaths. It didn't slow her heartbeat or the tremble in her hands. Taking the crystal from her pocket, she pressed it against the window. There was a soft popping sound and the window swung open. That was what she'd expected with the trinket box in Seren's room. Slipping the crystal into her pocket, she strode over to Brynn and tried to tug him out of the chair.

He pulled away from her. "Go. I'm slowing you down."

"I'm not going anywhere without you."

Brynn let her tug him to his feet. "Don't let them catch you. At least promise me that."

"I have no plans to be caught, but I'm still not going to leave you behind." She helped him across the room. "Think you can get out the window?"

"Yes. Once you're out."

Melody wanted to protest, but could see she'd be

wasting her time. "I'll wait outside for you." She threw a leg over the window ledge before looking back at him. "I'm not going anywhere without you." She finished climbing out the window. It took far longer for Brynn to climb out the window than she liked and she kept wanting to beg him to hurry. She remained silent, knowing he was probably moving as fast as possible. Her gaze was drawn to the dark veins raised on his arms. How long did he have before the poison killed him? She really needed to get him back to the Fae Court.

Brynn tumbled the rest of the way out of the window and landed sprawled on the ground at her feet. "Where's Sorrow?" He struggled to stand.

She helped him to his feet. "Uhmm." She tried to figure out where the back of the castle was. She really hoped she wasn't going to need to travel nearly all the way around the castle to find out where Sorrow was hidden. "This way." It seemed to be as good as taking the other direction.

The sky was starting to lighten when Melody spotted the clump of trees where she'd left Sorrow. Maybe they should have crossed the meadow first, but it had seemed quicker to travel around the castle before she headed into the forest. Her arm tightened around Brynn. "Think you can move any faster? I really don't want to be out in the open any longer than necessary."

"Go without me."

"Stop telling me that. Now hurry up." She drew him away from the shadows cast by the castle, wishing she could remain hidden there until the arachnids forgot about Brynn. She doubted that would happen any time soon. They seemed like the sort to hold a grudge forever.

Every single sound and movement had her jumping and turning in that direction. By the time they'd reached the safety of the forest she was a nervous wreck. If a spider had chosen that moment to appear, she probably would have screamed before fainting. Letting go of Brynn, she dropped the sword on the ground and wrapped her arms around Sorrow's neck, relieved he'd waited. It took her a moment to bring herself to let go of him. She removed her backpack. The sound of Brynn crashing to the ground had her dropping her backpack and kneeling at his side.

He tried to push her away. "I'm fine. We have to get out of here."

Instead of arguing with him that he didn't look fine, she took a bottle of water from her backpack and offered it to him. Her gaze was drawn to his shaking hands as he lifted the bottle for a drink. Her worry increased. He couldn't die. Not after all she'd gone through to get him out of there. The thought of losing him caused a sharp pain in her chest. He wasn't going to die.

Taking the bottle he held out, she had a drink before returning the bottle to the backpack, fixing up the straps so she could wear it. When she saw Brynn shivered, she took out the shirt she'd brought for him and helped him put it on.

She stared down at him. He looked worse. She slid her arms through the straps of the backpack and not knowing what else to do with the sword, she undid the belt she wore with her jeans and slid it through the loops of the scabbard. Buckling up her belt, she found it awkward to have a sword at her side. How did Brynn and all the other Fae who wore one make it look so natural? She tried to shift it into a more comfortable position.

"You need a shorter one."

She held out her hands and helped Brynn to his feet. "People don't wear swords in my world. Except for cosplay." She helped him onto the horse.

"When are you going home?"

She shrugged. The thought of going caused more pain than she'd expected it to. How could she stay in this world where giant spiders were a reality? "I don't know how to get back."

"If I wasn't so weak, I'd help you return home."

"Then I guess I need to find someone to heal you." She dragged herself onto Sorrow, the sword getting in the way several times.

"Take the shell, I gave you, to my castle and ask my knights to return you home."

She held onto him as Sorrow headed for the Fae Court. "No. I need to find someone who can help you."

"No one would do something like that for nothing. What are you willing to offer? It'll be you they'll expect to repay the favour for helping me because there's no guarantee I'll live. Not with how long the poison has been in my system."

"Shut up," she muttered. "You're not going to die."

It took less time for them to return to the light Fae Court as Sorrow went at a faster pace. Several times she nearly fell off, but that was only when Brynn started to drift off to sleep. It was after dark when they arrived and she was glad to see it was quiet around the stable. She rode Sorrow into his stall and fell off him when she attempted to dismount.

Melody glared up at Brynn when he chuckled. "I'd like to see you do any better at the moment." She muttered under her breath when he swung off the horse and staggered into the wall, but still kept his feet. "Wait here."

Getting to her feet, she strode through the stables trying to find someone. When she found one of the younger stablehands she asked him to send Carden to Sorrow's stall. She hurried back there, her heart lurching when she saw Brynn collapsed in the straw. She knelt at his side and pressed her hand against his chest. His heart beat weakly within him, but she could feel no warmth in his skin. A sound behind her had her spinning as she leapt to her feet, her hand going to the hilt of the sword. She breathed in an unsteady breath when she saw it was Carden.

Chapter Twenty-One

Carden glanced towards Brynn, but stood there silently, his arms folded across his chest.

"I need to get Brynn to his rooms without anyone seeing him," Melody said.

Carden remained silent.

She felt like growling in frustration. "What do you want in exchange?"

"More than the question you owe me."

She glanced around, trying to think what else she could offer him. Lifting her hand, she slowly turned it so he could see the many charms hanging from her bracelet. "I have another one of these in Brynn's room. A violin. The question and the violin charm are yours if you help me get Brynn there without others knowing."

He stared at her for a long drawn out moment before he nodded once and walked away.

She stared after him, wondering what he was doing and if she should follow. He returned with several old horse blankets and wrapped them around Brynn, who didn't even open his eyes. She followed Carden into the castle and through the numerous corridors. When she saw the door of Brynn's room she hurried ahead and opened it. She collected the gold charm while Carden put Brynn on his bed and gathered up the horse blankets.

Carden came out of the bedroom and took the charm, turning it in his fingers as he examined it. With a nod, he headed for the door.

"Thank you." She watched as he left, not even looking in her direction at her words. She closed the door behind him and went to check on Brynn. Pressing her palm against his cheek, she spoke his name softly. He didn't wake. "Brynn." Her tone was sharp this time.

He opened his eyes with several long, slow blinks. "How did I get in here?"

Relief had her smiling. "I'll be back soon. With help."

Brynn struggled to sit up. "I don't have any allies here. Don't let yourself be caught in an impossible obligation for me."

She pressed against his chest. "Stay here. I won't

be long." At least she hoped not. When he collapsed against his pillow again she headed for the door. She didn't want to leave him, but had no choice. Without help, he'd die. The veins were becoming bigger and darker, some small ones marring his cheeks. Stepping into the corridor, she blinked back tears. Reed would demand more if she let him know how important Brynn was to her.

Reaching his room, she knocked on the door. She was about to give up when he swung the door open and after checking the corridor, stepped back to let her in. She had no idea what to say to him. Begging would be the worst plan ever.

"If you've come to discuss our previous negotiations, you're too late. You were meant to be here yesterday morning."

"No, the other person I was negotiating with came through with a better offer." Why couldn't dealing with the Fae be easier than this? She didn't want Brynn to die, but she also didn't want to be stuck here as someone's pet for the rest of her life.

"What do you want? I have other plans for the evening."

She eyed him up and down. He didn't look like he was dressed to attend anything important. "Are you going somewhere?"

"What do you want?"

"I heard the queen is annoyed with Seren for losing the pink diamond necklace she was meant to return to her in fifty years' time."

Reed's eyes narrowed. "You have no hold over me." He started for the door. "I don't have time for this."

Panic rushed through her. He couldn't leave. She stepped in front of him. "I need a favour from you."

"I don't have time for doing favours."

"Brynn is dying. Dione poisoned him. I want you to take the poison from him." She could almost see him calculating what he could ask for.

"I need you to deliver something for me." He withdrew a velvet pouch from his pocket and tipped the contents into his palm.

She stared at the pink diamond. "If I do that, will you save him?"

"You'll also owe me five other favours I can claim when I wish."

At his words, her gaze flew to his. "Why?"

"Because the task I've asked of you is worth far less than saving a life."

She gestured towards the diamond. "You want me to risk my life. I thought you said you didn't want to steal the queen's necklace."

"This isn't hers."

"It was only temporarily Seren's. So technically, it still belonged to the queen."

"It was never the queen's in the first place."

She wanted to tell him to hurry up, but knew it was dangerous not to be careful when making bargains with the Fae. Look what had happened because of her mum's open ended bargain. "I thought you said the queen owns a pink diamond necklace like this one." She nodded towards his hand.

"She does. Hers is inferior to this one."

"Why don't you explain all this so I can understand it? Who does it belong to? How did the queen end up with it? And why did you want me to steal it from her?"

"It belonged to my sister about a century ago and has been in our family longer than that. The queen tricked my sister out of the necklace. When Seren managed to gain temporary ownership of the necklace I saw it as an opportunity to get it back for our family."

She noticed Reed had looked towards the door several times throughout their conversation. It seemed like she wasn't the only one in a hurry. "Someone suspects you, don't they?"

He dropped the necklace into the bag. "How could you even suggest that?"

She noticed he didn't deny it. "If I deliver the necklace you can remain here and out of suspicion. If you disappeared now, they'd instantly believe it was you. I'll deliver the necklace and do two other favours for you that it wouldn't pain me to do. You need my help more than I need yours."

"Without my help, Brynn will die."

She shook her head, not wanting to let him know how accurate his words were. "You're not the only one capable of healing around here. But I am one of the few who can leave without someone suspecting something."

He held the bag out to her. "I'll arrange for a horse that knows the way to my sister's home."

She took the bag and slipped it into her backpack she still wore. "I can't ride. You better make it an extremely quiet horse." She doubted he cared what happened to her. "It'd be a bad idea if I had an accident and someone else ended up with the diamond."

Reed nodded. "Where's Brynn?"

"In his room. I'll let you in." She led the way, glad the corridors were empty. When she reached Brynn's side, it took every ounce of willpower not to let Reed see how shocked she was by Brynn's condition. Large dark veins of poison snaked across his cheeks. She didn't speak for fear she'd beg Reed to hurry.

Reed stood beside Brynn, examining him. "Bring me a bowl or jug I can put the poison in. Something large."

She returned to the sitting room and took the jug that had once contained water. Giving it to Reed, she stepped back and watched. Several times she had to uncurl her fingers. She didn't want Reed to see how worried she was.

Reed held Brynn's hand above the jug and the room filled with the scent of cinnamon. The dark veins of poison travelled through his body towards his arm. Poison dripped from Brynn's fingertips and into the jug as the dark veins receded from the rest of his body to fill that one arm with ropes of black. Slowly they left his arm and once the last of the poison had dripped from Brynn's fingertips, Reed lowered it to the bed.

Melody took the jug Reed gave her, surprised it was nearly full. "Thank you."

"I'll take you to the stables."

"I need a few minutes before I'm ready. I'll meet you in your room."

Reed's gaze was momentarily drawn to her

backpack. "I wouldn't take too long if I was you. They've started randomly searching people."

Now he told her. "I won't be long."

He gestured towards Brynn. "He won't wake for several hours. His body needs to heal."

"I'll meet you in your room." She strode to the door leading to the corridor and opened it. Reed held her gaze for a moment before he nodded and left the room. She closed the door behind him, placed the jug on the coffee table and removed the sword from her belt before sinking into one of the armchairs. She was tired and exhausted and desperately needed sleep. But there was no time for any of that.

She slipped her arms out of the backpack straps and removed the bag containing the diamond necklace. Tipping it into her hand, she stared at it. She'd thought she'd seen the last of the diamond when she'd given it to Reed. She dropped it back into the bag and tucked it in one of her pockets. Her fingers brushed against the shell that was also in there.

She rose wearily to her feet and checked on Brynn. Although he was pale, he looked far healthier. She also couldn't see any streaks of poison running through his body. Forcing herself to turn away, she returned to the sitting room and found pen and paper to leave him a note. She warned him the jug contained poison, told him she had a small task she needed to complete and said she'd see him soon. She stared at the piece of paper with her messy scrawl, trying to think how to sign off. In the end she wrote 'Love Melody'. If he hadn't already realised that after all she'd done, he wasn't very smart. She had no idea how she was going to manage to leave him behind and return home. Staying in this realm wasn't an option. She had no idea how to survive here.

After checking Brynn one more time, she left her gear behind and headed to Reed's rooms. He rose from the armchair he'd been sitting in when she opened the door. "I'm ready to go."

Reed indicated the door. "You're no longer my protégée. In future you will knock."

She nodded. "How long will it take me to get to your sister's place?"

"Three or four hours."

"Okay." She could manage six to eight hours without her gear. It was probably better to travel light. "Lead the way." She gestured towards the door.

"Follow, but not too close. The less people who see you with me, the better."

She nodded and followed him into the corridor, letting him get well ahead of her. Several times she had to hurry when he turned a corner so she didn't risk losing him, but eventually they reached the stable without anyone stopping either of them. She waited for him in the stable courtyard and when he brought out a saddled white horse, followed him to a shadowy area.

Reed held out the reins to her. "Tell her to go home and she'll take you to the back door of my sister's place."

She took the reins. "What's your sister's name?"

"Aderyn. Do you need help on the horse?"

Melody nodded. Once she was seated, she asked, "How do I get back here?"

"Tell the horse to return." Reed strode away.

Melody stared after him, worried there was more information she might have needed. A movement caught her attention and she saw someone slip through the shadows, following Reed. Lantern light fell on them for a second and her mouth dropped open when she saw it was Noah. What was he doing? She had no time to stay and find out. She needed to see Aderyn and get back before she fell asleep on the horse. That wouldn't go well. She was barely able to remain seated when she was awake.

"Go home." Her hands tightened on the reins as the horse moved off. After a bit, she relaxed and eventually nodded off to sleep, coming abruptly awake when she nearly fell from the horse. She had no idea how long it took to reach Aderyn's home. Several times she nodded off, coming awake to grab at the saddle as she started to slip sideways. When the horse finally stopped at the back door of a cottage surrounded by flowering shrubs, it was still night. She slid off the horse, actually managing to remain on her feet.

Her smile faded when she faced the door that was well lit by lanterns that hung nearby. Was Reed's sister expecting her? Would she be pleased or horrified to be given the necklace? Straightening her shoulders, she closed the distance between her and the door and knocked sharply on the timber. The sound was greeted by silence. What if Aderyn wasn't home? She knocked again.

Chapter Twenty-Two

"Can I help you?"

Melody spun to see a young woman standing behind her. She was tall and slim and had the same white-blond hair that Reed had. "Are you Aderyn?"

"Yes. Who are you?"

"Your brother sent me."

"Which brother?"

"Reed." She hadn't realised he had more than one sibling. "He asked me to bring you something." She glanced towards the door, uncomfortable with showing her the necklace where anyone might see, even though it was unlikely anyone else was about. "Can we go inside?"

Aderyn nodded and stepped past her to open the door. "What has Reed sent me?"

Melody stepped into the dim interior, only a single lantern providing light, and waited until Aderyn closed the door before she drew the bag from her pocket. When her fingers brushed against the shell she thought of Brynn and wondered if he was awake yet. Had he found her letter? She tipped the necklace into her hand.

Aderyn gasped. "He didn't."

"Not exactly. But he did organise it."

Aderyn reached for the diamond, stopping before she could touch. "May I?"

Melody nodded.

Aderyn took the necklace and held it close to examine it. "He did. Why would he do this? No one can know."

Melody shrugged.

"You won't say anything? Will you?" Aderyn lowered her hand.

"All Reed asked me to do was deliver the necklace. I've done that. Now I need to go. I've got other things I need to do." She tried not to yawn, but it was impossible to stop. She pressed her hand against her mouth.

"I'm sorry. I didn't even think to ask if you wanted refreshments or to take a rest before you continue your journey."

"I'm fine. Thank you though." She held out the bag

to Aderyn. "Is there something I can stand on to make it easier to get on the horse?"

Aderyn took the bag and slipped the necklace inside it. "Yes. There's a large stone around the side of the house. I'll show you." Aderyn removed the lantern from its hook and led the way outside.

Melody took the reins of the horse and followed Aderyn around the house to the rock. She used it to clamber awkwardly onto the horse. "Thank you." Again she tried to stifle a yawn. Again she failed.

"Are you sure you don't want to rest before you continue your journey? It isn't always safe to travel at night."

Melody shook her head. "I'm fine." She wanted to return home before something else happened. If Reed wanted his last two favours completed he could come to her in the human world to ask for them.

Aderyn held up the bag with the necklace in it. "Thank you. Tell Reed I fear he's spent too much time at court over the years. It's addled his brain." She grinned before lowering her hand.

With a nod, Melody spoke to the horse. "Return." She was relieved when the horse headed in the direction they'd come from. The journey back to the court was as tedious as the one from Dione's castle. She kept nodding off to sleep and nearly falling from the horse before she was jarred awake. The fifth time she did it, the horse reared and she slid off, landing on the hard ground. She glared at the horse that was prancing about. What had got into the beast? A rustle in nearby bushes had the horse rearing again. This time when the hooves hit the ground, the horse raced off into the night.

Melody swore, rising to her feet and dusting off the seat of her jeans. She eyed the bushes where the rustle had come from. Everything was quiet there. Not knowing what else she could do, she continued along the track the horse had been following. Luckily it was clear enough to see in the limited light cast by the moon. Although that would probably change once she left the meadow, she was currently travelling through, and reached the dense forest she could see further up the track.

Withdrawing the shell Brynn had given her, she pressed it to her lips. "Brynn." She didn't know if he was well enough to come after her or even if he'd be able to find her, but she had to do something. She was probably still an hour's ride away from the castle. She didn't know for certain since she'd kept falling asleep. At least the fall from the horse had woken her. A sound off to her right had her looking in that direction. She saw nothing.

Lengthening her stride, she continued walking along the track, raising the shell to her lips again. "Brynn." Did he have to be awake to hear her calling him? She had no idea how it worked. This time a sound to her left drew her attention. What was making the noises? It was worse not being able to see. She tried to tell herself it was probably something little, like a rabbit, but she struggled to believe. Her imagination went wild and she came up with all sorts of creatures, including ones that had her shuddering and walking faster. Any faster and she'd be running.

This time the sound was behind her. She glanced over her shoulder and stumbled. There were shadows behind her on either side of the track. Probably shrubs. Hopefully. Hearing how fast she was breathing, she tried to slow it down. Instead she gave up and broke into a run, wanting to get back as quickly as possible. She continued to clutch the shell in her hand and considered whispering Brynn's name against it once again.

A sound ahead of her drew her gaze and she nearly tripped over her own feet when she saw the darkened shape of an arachnid slip into the forest. Behind her was another noise and she turned to find an arachnid closing in on her. She froze, her hand tightening on the shell. She had to move. There was no way she wanted that arachnid to come any closer. At another sound behind her, she looked over her shoulder to see the other arachnid had come out of the forest and onto the track. The two were closing in on her.

With a ragged gasp, she raced off to her right, having no idea where she was going or what she'd find. All she knew was that the arachnids looked like they were there for her. She heard them getting closer and veered towards the forest. Maybe she could lose them amongst the trees. Anything was worth a try. She tried to run faster and not think about what was behind her for fear she'd freeze.

It didn't take her long to realise the forest wasn't a good place to run through in the dark. She crashed into trees, stumbled over objects and jumped at every sound. Slowing down, she tried to figure out where the arachnids were. They were far more silent than she was. Pressing the shell to her lips, she whispered Brynn's name against it then dropped it onto the ground and stomped on it. She felt the shell break and hoped Brynn found her before the arachnids did. She didn't like her chances. Nor did she know if he was well enough to come after her. How quickly did magic help someone heal? She had no idea.

Trying to remain quiet, she moved through the forest, her hands outstretched in the hope that she didn't keep running into things. She had to find somewhere to hide. She couldn't keep crashing through the forest. They'd eventually find her. A darker patch near the ground appeared in front of her and her heart leapt before she realised it was a shrub. She froze, listening for the arachnids. She couldn't hear them or see them. Not that she could see much in the forest. Crouching, she pushed herself into the middle of the shrub, the branches catching at her hair and scratching her face and hands.

She huddled against the earth, the smell of dirt and old leaves wafting around her. Feeling thirsty, she both regretted not bringing her backpack and was relieved she didn't have it so she was able to hide easier. Where were the arachnids? Surely they weren't capable of walking that quietly through the forest. She started to slip her fingers into her pocket then stopped, reminding herself the shell was smashed somewhere on the forest floor. She hadn't managed to keep it for much longer than she'd kept the worry stone.

She had no idea how much time had passed when her foot started to go to sleep and she struggled to move without making a sound, trying to wriggle her toes. She managed to shift sideways and put out a hand to take some of her weight. There was a snap as a twig broke beneath her hand. She held her breath, trying to ignore the sensation coming back to her feet.

"Pirro? Did you hear that?"

She breathed shallowly, not wanting to pass out.

"No. What was it?"

"I think I heard the girl. Over this way."

The arachnid's voice sounded closer. She didn't recognise it.

"Maybe you should go for reinforcements. If we don't catch the girl, Dione is likely to kill both of us," Pirro said.

"I can't believe a human thought she could get away with stealing our prisoner."

How had they known? Did they have spy cams in their dungeon? No, that didn't make sense. Technology didn't work properly here. The hand she leaned on started to get pins and needles, but she wasn't game to move even slightly.

"Bring back reinforcements. Twenty knights should be enough."

She could have sworn her heart briefly stopped at the thought of twenty-two arachnids scouring the forest for her. She couldn't stay here. As soon as they moved away from this area she had to try and escape.

"I'll see you in a couple of hours, Pirro."

Even though she strained to listen, she didn't hear a single sound. How would she know when Pirro had moved away? She slowly counted to a hundred in her head. Was that enough time? She shifted slightly, holding her breath as if that would prevent her from making a noise. When her movement remained undetected she moved a little bit further.

She didn't even know what time it was or how long before daybreak arrived. Or for that matter, where she was. She left the safety of the shrub and peered around, remaining crouched beside it. Was it a little less dark? She had no idea. She slowly stood up, her gaze darting in every direction. Pirro could be anywhere. She crept through the forest, heading in a direction that seemed to be less shadowy.

With every step, she glanced around trying to make sense of her surroundings. If only it wasn't so dark. When a branch cracked beneath her step, she froze. Scanning her surroundings she could see no movement. Taking a bigger step, she cringed at the slight snapping a twig made. She closed her eyes, her breath shuddering in and out as she tried to stop panic from washing over her.

With a deep breath, she opened her eyes and took a step forward. She could do this. Another step. She wasn't about to stay here until Pirro found her. No way. Another glance around followed by another step. Dawn was definitely coming because the shadows weren't as deep anymore.

One step after another, her heart pounding in her ears, the seconds becoming minutes, the shadows changing from black to grey. When she came to the edge of the forest she reached out to rest her hand against the trunk of a tree, the solidness comforting. She was on the banks of a flowing stream. Thirst drew her forward several steps before she thought to check her surroundings. There was no one around and she darted forward, kneeling on the ground to cup handfuls of water to her mouth.

"Don't make this hard on yourself."

Spinning, she landed sprawled on the dirt at the water's edge. Pirro stood several metres from her, drawing two daggers.

"Dione wants you brought to her alive. It's up to you what condition you reach her in."

Her breath came fast and she awkwardly backed away from him, her hands skimming the dirt as she searched for something to use as a weapon. There was only dirt and occasionally pebbles and leaves. "How did you find me?"

"Eolande's pet told us where you were going and

that you brought Brynn back." Pirro took several steps towards her.

It looked like she'd been right to worry about Noah wanting revenge. She continued to search the ground for something to use against Pirro. There was nothing but dirt. He continued to come closer until he was standing over her, still holding his daggers. Her hands tightened around clumps of dirt, her body frozen as her gaze zoomed in on the spider legs towering over her.

"You can't escape. Give up."

Chapter Twenty-Three

Pirro's words reminded her of how Elon hadn't thought she'd last a week without being hopelessly tangled in the realms of the Fae. Closing her eyes, she flung both handfuls of dirt at Pirro. He swore and cursed and something heavy thunked down beside her. When dirt stopped raining down upon her, she opened her eyes to see one of his daggers lying in the dirt, Pirro still swearing. Grabbing hold of the dagger, she scrambled to her feet, running for the forest, her breath coming in uneven gasps.

"You'll pay for that."

Pirro's threat rang out behind her as he continued to curse her. She kept going, not even checking over her shoulder to see if he followed. She didn't want to risk running into anything. Heading for where the trees grew thicker and the shadows were deeper, she didn't stop until trees surrounded her. Turning, she searched the area, unable to see Pirro anywhere. Was he still following her or did he plan to wait for reinforcements? Continuing to look around, she crept through the closely growing trees. She tried to slow her breathing down, but every little sound had her gasping and spinning towards it.

She had no idea which direction to take. She was hopelessly lost and feared she'd never find a way back to the light Fae Court. Slipping between two closely growing trees she pressed a hand against her mouth to prevent a scream from escaping. Her other hand tightened on the handle of the dagger, her gaze focused on the figure in front of her.

"I warned you."

She tried to back away from Pirro, but ran into a tree. Raising the dagger, she tried not to look at his legs. As long as she focused only on his face she might be able to trick herself into believing he wasn't part spider. "You're not taking me to Dione." Just because the arachnid queen wanted her alive didn't mean she planned to keep her that way.

Pirro chuckled. "Do you think you stand a chance against me? I might not be as powerful as the Fae, but I'm not as weak as a human."

She didn't know if she stood a chance, but giving up would kill her. "Does fly spray kill you like a normal spider?" When he leapt at her with a growl, she began to wonder if she should have remained silent. Throwing herself to the side, she barely managed not to scream when her arm brushed against his leg. A shudder went through her as she scrambled to her feet and ran blindly through the forest.

A scream did escape when a web wrapped around her arm and pulled her to a stumbling halt. She slashed at it with the dagger, turning to face Pirro when the web broke. Continuing to hold the dagger in front of her, she backed away from him. Keeping her gaze on his face she tried to forget he was part spider. Every time she thought of it or looked at his legs, she froze for a second. If she wanted to survive she needed to get past her fear. Hadn't she managed to wear that dress Elon had given her? She wondered what had happened to it.

"When Dione is finished with you, I'm going to feed you to my children."

Another shudder went through her as images of miniature Pirros with large fangs came to mind, even though none of the arachnids she'd seen had fangs. She pushed the images from her mind so she could keep moving.

"Even if you get past me, it won't be long before the forest is full of arachnid knights."

His words had her freezing again and she had to force herself to keep moving. She backed into another tree and stepped to the side, trying to get past it. The bark scraped against her back through her t-shirt and she began to wonder how big the tree was. She couldn't bring herself to look. That would mean taking her gaze away from Pirro.

"Not that you'll make much of a meal for the four of them."

Coming to the edge of the tree she stumbled. Her grip tightened on the dagger she continued to hold in front of her. She had no idea what to do. Running didn't seem like it'd help. Nor did she want to turn her back on him when he was so close.

Pirro attacked, his dagger slashing towards her. The only reason he missed was because she fell over. She struck out at him with the dagger she'd taken. It sliced into his leg and dark liquid gushed over her hand. When he roared and attacked her again, she scrambled around the tree, blindly waving the dagger. On the other side of the tree she heard him cursing and threatening her. The words made her shudder and want to freeze so she tried not to listen to them. Not far off she heard the sound of hoof beats, feeling the vibration in the ground.

Pirro laughed. "It won't matter now. Can't you

hear my knights? They're nearly here and you'll be trussed and taken back to Dione."

She wasn't about to stand around waiting for them. Running through the forest, she came out at the bank again, tumbling into the water. The cold stream had her gasping for breath and she struggled through the running water to the other side. Her gasps turned into sobs as she heard the sounds of the horses coming closer. Reaching the other bank she stumbled, landing sprawled on the ground. She heard them entering the water, and tried to rise, the dagger clutched tightly in her hand.

"Melody!"

She froze, certain she was hearing things. Looking over her shoulder she saw Brynn swing down off Sorrow and wade through the stream to her. Behind him were eight Fae, two females in the group. Some were mounted on black horses, others on white. They all looked like they were part light and part dark Fae like Brynn was. "Brynn?"

He grinned, dragging her to her feet and wrapping his arms around her. "When you crushed the shell I was terrified." His arms tightened. The scent of his magic washed over her, drying her clothes and healing the scratches on her arms and face.

"Me too." She pulled back slightly. "How did you find me?"

He held up his hand, a thread of her hair wrapped around his wrist. "I traced you."

"How did your knights know to come?"

"I sent a message for them before I left in case something happened. They were to meet me on the road. When I wasn't there, they searched for me before going to the light Fae Court."

She started to ask him another question when she remembered that twenty-one arachnid knights would soon be joining Pirro. "We've got to get out of here. Pirro has reinforcements coming."

"Not anymore."

His tone and the hard look on his face frightened her. "You killed them?"

"Would you have preferred that they killed us?"

She shook her head. "Of course not. I just…" Her voice trailed off when she couldn't think what to say. "What about Pirro?"

"If he's smart, he didn't stick around."

Pirro hadn't struck her as being stupid. "Noah told them."

Brynn nodded once. "Let's get you back to the Fae Court. You look exhausted." He took the dagger from her and handed it to one of his knights.

When she was seated before him on Sorrow, she turned her head so she could see him. "You're not going to kill Noah, are you?"

"He's the queen's pet."

"That didn't answer my question."

"The queen would be upset if someone harmed her pet."

She opened her mouth to ask if that meant Noah was safe, but closed it instead. She thought of how Reed had waited for so long to take his family's pink diamond back. Noah would be safe as long as he remained the queen's pet.

Exhaustion and the movement of the horse had her falling asleep. She woke to find herself being handed down to one of Brynn's knights. He helped her stand and she looked around, surprised to find it was early morning and they were at the stables. Brynn joined her and slid an arm around her waist. She leaned against him, wanting to sleep for the rest of the day.

"Are you fine?"

She walked beside him towards the castle. "I should be the one asking that. I was worried you'd die."

Brynn chuckled. "So was I."

"That's not amusing. How do you feel?" She glanced behind at the six knights following them.

The other two had stayed behind to deal with the horses.

"Fine. What do you owe Reed?"

She shrugged. "I don't know."

Brynn stopped abruptly and faced her, grabbing hold of her shoulders. "You entered an open bargain? Are you crazy?" His hands tightened on her.

Glaring, she drew away from him. "What was I meant to do? Let you die?"

"What did you agree to?"

She was conscious of the knights watching them. "I'm tired. Can't we talk about this later?

He nodded. "Sorry. Of course you are." He let go of her shoulders and slid his arm around her waist again. He remained silent as they strode through the corridors.

When they were close to Brynn's rooms, Melody spotted Noah turning a corner ahead of them. "I won't be a minute. I have to do something." She glanced behind them. "Without your entourage." She raced down the corridor before he could speak, turning in the direction Noah had taken, forcing her exhausted body to move faster than it wanted to. She saw him ahead of her. "Noah!"

He faced her, quickly masking the look of surprise

that crossed his face. He glanced over his shoulder. "I can't stand around talking. I'm running late."

"This won't take long."

Noah looked over her shoulder before meeting her gaze. "We have nothing to talk about." Again he glanced over her shoulder.

Having a good idea why he kept looking past her, she checked. At the end of the corridor Brynn stood with his arms crossed over his chest, his knights behind him with hands resting on the hilts of the swords they wore at their sides. She sighed. Not quite what she was wanting when she'd said without his entourage. She faced Noah. "They told me." She kept her voice low.

"I have no idea what you're talking about."

"Dione's knights." It was a lot easier than saying arachnids.

Noah took a step away from her. "You forced me to take sides in that fight. I had to show I wasn't with you."

"Really? Are you declaring yourself my enemy?"

He looked past her again, shaking his head. "No. Of course not."

She smiled. She'd obviously been hanging around the Fae far too long. "No? Then I guess you're looking for a way to prove you're not my enemy.

You could go to Reed and tell him you'd like to take responsibility for the two favours I owe him."

Shaking his head Noah took another step back from her, a nervous glance over her shoulder. "Of course I don't want to do that."

She shrugged, her smile fading. "I suppose that's your answer then. I'll let Brynn know." She started to turn away.

Noah reached out, grabbing hold of her arm so she couldn't turn fully. "Wait."

Melody saw Brynn's hand go to his sword and he took a step towards them. She bit back a smile when Noah let go of her arm. Meeting Brynn's gaze, she shook her head slightly before she faced Noah. "What?"

"I'll," he swallowed heavily. "I'll see him."

"Tell Reed I want him to tell me personally whether or not he accepts your offer." When Noah nodded, she strode back to Brynn. She rested her hand on his chest. "Don't harm him."

"Ever?"

She thought about it. It wouldn't be fair to leave him hampered by promises when she returned to her own world. "Not yet. Let's see what he does."

He took her hand, tangling his fingers in hers.

"What have you done?" They walked towards his rooms.

"I'm not sure yet. Hopefully dealt with favours I really didn't want to repay." They reached his rooms and she was glad the knights remained outside.

"What favours?"

It was probably going to be a much longer conversation than she was up to dealing with right now. "I need sleep."

For a moment Brynn looked like he was going to argue, then he nodded. "Sleep."

"Wake me if Reed comes to see me." She started to move away from him.

He tugged her back, wrapping his arms around her and kissing her before he let her go. "What are you planning?"

"Going home." The words came out sounding more like an apology and made her heart ache. But she couldn't stay. It wasn't possible. Look at all that had happened and she hadn't even been here a fortnight. Surviving a lifetime would be near impossible. She didn't have the skills needed to survive in this realm.

Brynn stared at her, finally nodding and turning away.

She wanted to reach out and draw him close.

Reassure him. Anything to remove the flash of hurt she'd seen in his eyes. Instead she grabbed a change of clothes and made her way to the bathroom, washing before dropping into the bed and falling instantly asleep.

Chapter Twenty-Four

Melody felt like it was no time at all before Brynn was waking her. She blinked up at him.

"Reed is here." He glanced over his shoulder.

She struggled to wake up, knowing she needed to be completely alert to deal with Reed. "Okay. I'll be out in a minute." She sat up and swung her legs over the edge of the bed, yawning.

Brynn looked at her for a moment before he nodded and left the room, closing the door behind him.

She stared at the closed door, feeling awkward. She kept feeling like she should apologise to him for wanting to go home. This wasn't her world. It was too dangerous a place for a human. Particularly one with no special talent. She thought of Noah who'd gained the attention of Eolande. Not that her attention had done him much good. He spent all his time trying to keep it.

Rising to her feet, she stretched then headed for the sitting room. She stopped just inside the room, noticing it was only Reed and Brynn inside. She wondered where Brynn's knights were. Surely he hadn't made them stay in the corridor. "Did Noah talk to you?"

"Yes."

"And?"

Reed turned to Brynn. "Have you considered teaching her how to ask questions?"

Brynn smiled. "It might be your lack of understanding that is the problem. I thought it was very clear that she wanted to know the results of the conversation."

Melody fought the urge to smile, wishing she could ask him if he'd known what she was asking or was asking the question she should have asked. "Well? What's the results?"

"I've chosen to accept Noah's favours in exchange for yours. He has a better understanding of how these things work."

Again she had to keep from smiling. "My obligations to you are done?"

Reed nodded, the scent of cinnamon momentarily

filling the room. "Was that all you wanted to see me about?"

"Yeah."

With a nod for Brynn, Reed left.

Melody caught a glimpse of several knights standing guard in the corridor. As soon as the door was closed she turned to Brynn, words failing her.

Brynn crossed the distance between them, drawing a bracelet from his pocket. "This shell might be easier to keep with you." He slipped it on her wrist.

She stared down at it. In the middle of the bracelet was a shell in a herringbone setting, a small pearl on either side of it. She brushed her fingers over the shell. "Is this to call you?"

"Yes." He reached out and ran his fingers through her hair, tangling them in the strands at the back of her head. "Do you still want to go home?"

She couldn't speak. Nodding, she blinked back the tears that wanted to fall.

"Are you sure?"

"I have to." Her words were a broken whisper.

"If you change your mind." He glanced at the bracelet.

"Brynn–"

He pressed a finger against her lips. "Stay with me till morning?"

She nodded, her lips meeting his when he lowered his head.

*   *   *

When morning arrived, she was no closer to being ready to leave. But she had to. It wasn't safe for her here. Brynn took her to the stream where she'd washed apples and filled water bottles. It seemed like so long ago now. Getting off Sorrow, they left behind the four knights that had followed them. Walking along the stream, her backpack not much lighter than the day she'd arrived, she couldn't stop thinking about the first time he'd brought her here. It had also been the first time she'd heard him laugh.

"Why here?"

Brynn half smiled. "My magic is stronger near water. Stronger still near the sea."

She traced his lips. "That was a perfectly good question."

"Barely." His smile faded. "Are you certain you wish to go home?"

She nodded. "I can't stay here." She thought of Dione. There was always the possibility she'd want to retaliate. It wasn't like she had a bunch of knights who could protect her like Brynn did. He should be safe now he had his knights with him. "I have to go home."

The scent of summer breezes and beaches filled the air and Brynn held out his closed hand, opening it to reveal a shell. "Rest your hand on it and think of your home."

She did as he said, trying to see it clearly. It took far longer than she expected. In the end she pictured the armchair in her mum's study pressed between two towering and cluttered bookcases. She'd sat in it so many times over the years. "Okay." The word was a whisper.

The scent of Brynn's magic rose around them and his lips met hers, his hand tightening over her hand so the shell was pressed between their palms.

She felt the shell break, but didn't pull away from him, continuing to cling to him even when the world shifted around them and she was home again. When he started to draw away from her, she tightened her arms around him. "Will I see you again?"

Brynn grinned, lifting her arm with the shell bracelet. "When you call me."

"You can come here?"

"I can't stay here long, but yes, I can visit you here."

"Why can't you stay for long?"

"Too much iron in your world." He stared at her a moment. "When you call me I'll come to your location. Make sure it's somewhere I can arrive without having to make numerous humans forget I appeared out of nowhere."

She nodded.

"Will you be safe if I leave you?"

Again she nodded.

He drew a sheathed dagger from the side of his boot. "This is yours."

She took it. "I don't know how to use it."

A grin momentarily appeared. "That's not what I've heard."

Her grip tightened on the dagger as she tried not to think about cutting Pirro. It hadn't been planned.

"Goodbye, Melody."

His words sounded so final. She wanted to beg him to take her back with him. Instead she threw her arms around him and kissed him once more before pulling away and running from the study, her vision blurred.

"Melody!"

She froze, dashing tears from her eyes. "Mum. You look terrible."

Sherry raced towards her, throwing her arms around her. "I can't believe you're here. It's only the start of March. Why are you here? What did you promise to come back for a visit?"

"It's not a visit. The obligation is paid."

Sherry held her at arm's length. "Are you okay? They didn't hurt you?"

She thought of Dione. "No."

"What's wrong?"

"I'm tired." And she missed Brynn already.

"How long were you there?"

"Today was the eleventh day." It had seemed far longer.

"You didn't eat their food?"

She pulled away from her mum. "I'm fine. What's been happening here? You said it's the start of March?"

"Yes. Oh Melody, you can't imagine how worried I've been." She reached for her. "I kept hoping to hear from you again."

Melody stepped away. "I need a shower."

Sherry's arms dropped to her side. "Of course."

Melody stood awkwardly in front of her mum for a moment. Somehow she'd expected her homecoming to be different. "Well." She gestured towards her room, conscious of the dagger still in her other hand. "I better..."

"Yes, of course."

Melody walked to her room, a glance over her shoulder before she stepped inside. She dropped her backpack and dagger on the floor as she closed the door, sliding down it to sit beside them. Silent tears fell and she tried not to make a sound. She should be happy. She'd escaped the realms of the Fae and only months had passed, not years. Closing her eyes she rubbed the shell of the bracelet, unable to stop thinking about Brynn. After several minutes she forced herself to rise and gather clothes, heading to the bathroom. Her mum was no longer in the hallway, but she'd left her study door open as an invitation.

When she came out of the bathroom, she found her mum waiting for her. She was tempted to ask what she wanted, but didn't really want to know. All she wanted to do was hide in her room and stop feeling like she'd left part of herself behind.

"I need to call your father and tell him you're back."

"Can we wait until tomorrow?"

Sherry shook her head.

"Until tonight?"

"I'll give you a couple of hours."

Melody sighed. He wasn't going to be happy. "Okay." She stepped around her mum and headed for her room, still feeling awkward and out of place. Obviously she needed to get used to her world again.

When her dad arrived, she quickly realised unhappy was an understatement. In the end she'd stormed to her room, slamming the door and locking it. Why had she returned? Her fingers brushed against the shell. If it weren't for extremely large spiders, Fae who wanted power over others and rules she had no clue about, she would have stayed. She smiled wryly. In other words a completely different world. Sighing, she crossed the room and turned on her laptop. She supposed she should let her friends know she was back. Her gaze was drawn to the dagger she'd placed beside the laptop earlier. Picking it up she drew it from the sheath, staring at the light reflecting off it. If only she'd known how to protect herself. She'd been too unprepared for Brynn's world.

Chapter Twenty-Five

By the time Melody had been back for a week she'd begun to think she didn't belong in the human world. Her friends treated her like an oddity and all of them seemed so shallow after the life and death events she'd become accustomed to dealing with. Her dad kept dropping in to see her and wanting to know what she planned to do with her life and school seemed like an alien environment that she no longer understood. Several times during the week she'd found herself searching online for horse riding lessons and self-defence classes before reminding herself she no longer needed them.

She'd also re-read her mum's books, unable to resist. They'd made her think of Brynn. Even eating apples brought him to mind. She'd returned her mum's bracelet, relieved she hadn't needed to part with a single charm. Returning it had brought more questions she hadn't been able to answer. Not without bursting into tears over everything she'd left behind.

She arrived home after school and strode through the hallway to her room. Each day of the past week had felt like a year. Partway along she saw a huntsman spider. She stopped, surprised that for once she wasn't frozen to the spot. It seemed so small and insignificant. Nothing like facing down Pirro.

Sherry came out of her study. "I thought I heard you–" She broke off as her gaze fell on the spider. "I'll grab the spray. It's okay."

"I'm fine. I can take care of it." She headed to the kitchen where the spray was kept under the sink. The spider was still there when she returned.

Sherry looked between her and the spider. "Let me take care of it for you." She held out her hand for the spray.

"I'm fine," Melody repeated.

The spider ran towards her when she sprayed him and even though her heart leapt and she jumped out of the way, she still managed to keep moving without freezing or going into a panic.

Sherry watched her. "What happened in the realms of the Fae?"

"Nothing." She headed for the kitchen, stepping

around the spider curled up on the floor. She hadn't been able to talk about her time there. Hadn't wanted to share it with anyone. None of them could have understood, not even her mum who'd been dealing with Elon for twenty years. Besides, thinking about it made her throat ache and tears threaten to fall. Speaking of it would have been impossible.

Sherry followed her. "Don't keep giving me that. There's no way you'd have got over your fear of spiders without something major having occurred."

She put the spray back under the sink and stared out the window. "Nothing happened." Her fingers rubbed absently against the shell. She couldn't stop thinking about all the good moments. Most of them involved Brynn. It finally dawned on her, even without any skills, she'd survived in the realms of the Fae.

"Who gave you the bracelet?"

She faced her mum, her gaze momentarily drawn to the charm bracelet she'd returned not long after she'd arrived home. The word 'home' rang falsely. How had it taken this long for her to realise? "I'm going back."

"What?"

Melody smiled, the first time she'd felt like doing so since arriving. "I'm going back."

"Why?"

She chuckled, thinking of how Brynn would have complained about her mum's inability to ask a proper question. "Because I don't belong here anymore."

"What happened there?"

"Nothing." Her smile remained in place. "And everything."

"This is all to do with a boy. I recognise that look. Is he human?"

"No."

"You're not going."

Once her mum's announcement would have made her angry. "I'm sorry, but I can't stay." Even facing Pirro had been better than the colourless life she was now living.

"You ate their food, didn't you? That's why you've been moping around the place."

She shook her head. "No. It's because I never should have left in the first place. Actually, I didn't leave, I ran away." She'd let a strange world and fear keep her from Brynn and a life that would be far more interesting than this one. She ran her fingers over the shell.

"Is that from him?"

"Yeah. For when I want to call him."

"How old is he?"

Laughter bubbled up as she recalled her own worries about that. "Barely a year older than me." She sobered. "I can't stay here." This time it didn't hurt to speak the words. She should have realised she was making the wrong decision from the pain it had caused her to make it.

"I want to meet him."

"You can, but even if you hate him I won't be staying."

"What about your father? Are you planning on running off again and leaving only a note?"

She shook her head. "No. I'll ring him." It was the last thing she wanted to do, but he didn't deserve her running off without an explanation of some kind. He'd probably be straight over and lecture her non-stop.

"What's his name?"

"Brynn." She needed to speak his name against the shell. Impatience had her wanting to hurry her mum up so she could retreat to her room. She wanted to be alone when she called him.

"When are you going?"

She shrugged. "I don't know." She wished she could leave now. "Soon."

"I don't want you to go. You're still a child."

She didn't feel like one. Not after everything that had happened. "I know."

"But you're going anyway, aren't you?"

"Yeah." She couldn't wait any longer. She started to walk past her mum.

"Melody?" Sherry waited until she faced her. "What happened?"

A smile slowly formed. Maybe one day she'd tell her mum. She might even let her write a story about it. "Everything." She strode to her room, closing and locking the door before she brought her bracelet to her lips. "Brynn." She waited, wanting to tell him to hurry. When he appeared in front of her, the scent of his magic fading, she threw herself at him. "I want to go home."

Brynn held her tight. "From that statement I take it this isn't home."

"It isn't now. I missed you."

"I noticed. You kept interrupting my sleep last night and I was beginning to think sleep would be impossible again tonight."

"That's it? That's all the time that's passed? I only left you yesterday?"

"What do you mean by all? It was an eternity."

"A week was an eternity."

"Then come home with me now."

"I can't."

"I thought-"

She pressed her fingers against his lips. "You have to promise to teach me how to ride and how to find my way with the castle ceiling lights. And how to look after myself." She glanced towards the dagger that she kept on her desk. "I don't want to be so unprepared this time. I need to be able to take care of myself."

"I'll always protect you, but I can teach you." The scent of his magic filled the room. "And I can give you something even better than lessons in fighting." He held out his hand. It appeared to be filled with sand, glints of light glittering and sparkling amongst the ordinary looking grains.

She breathed in deeply. She'd missed the smell of summer breezes and beaches. "What is it?"

"Fae magic." He held her gaze. "If you take it, you can never turn back. This world will never truly be yours again."

She giggled. "Fairy dust?" She giggled again at the look he gave her.

"No. Fae magic. I have to warn you it'll make it harder for you to lie."

She grinned at his comment before becoming serious and holding out her hand. "I understand. I'm not interested in this world. It hasn't been mine since the moment I left." When the sand poured into her hand, she stared down at it. The sensation of it touching her palm felt almost like pins and needles and the sand sank into her skin the moment it made contact. The smell of vanilla rose up around her and she breathed in the scent of her magic. "You won't miss this amount of magic?" The pins and needles sensation felt like it travelled through her body, causing goosebumps to rise.

He grinned. "It'll return over time, just like your own will become more powerful." He paused. "Can we go home now?"

She shook her head. "Not this second. You have to meet my mum and I need to say goodbye to my dad. But I couldn't wait any longer to see you."

"Let's get it over and done with so we can return home. I told my knights we'd travel to my castle tomorrow."

It was odd to think she'd be living in a castle. She smiled. Life was going to be far more interesting in the realms of the Fae. "I need you to do one more thing first before you meet my mum."

"You're asking for even more favours?"

Melody laughed at his expression of disbelief. "I think this is a favour you're going to want to do."

"What makes you so certain of that?"

"Kiss me."

Disbelief was replaced with anticipation. "That's a favour I'm always willing to owe you." His lips met hers.

She held him tight, returning his kiss. She had no idea what a future in the realms of the Fae would be like, but it had to be better than a future without entanglements.

Free Ebook

Sign up to Avril's newsletter to receive a free ebook. This ebook is exclusive to those on her mailing list. To find out more about this offer visit: http://www.avrilsabine.com/free-ebook/

*

We value your privacy and will not sell, rent, exchange or loan your email address to third parties. Your information is confidential and you are under no obligation to remain on the mailing list and can unsubscribe at any time.

Acknowledgements

As always, thanks to the usual crew and a special thanks to Cat. I absolutely love the cover of this book.

To The Reader

If you enjoyed this book, why not consider leaving a review to help other readers discover it too? Reader engagement is one of the few ways that lets an author know readers want more books in a particular series or genre. So leave a review and tell friends, not only about this book but also about other ones you've enjoyed, so you can continue to enjoy books by your favourite authors for years to come.

Dreams are meant to be lived,

Avril.

About The Author

Avril is an Australian fiction writer who lives with her family on acreage in South East Queensland. She writes mostly young adult speculative fiction, but has been known to dabble in other genres. You can find more information about her at her website www.avrilsabine.com where you can also sign up for her newsletter to be kept informed about new releases, current projects, blog posts and exclusive news.

Titles By Avril Sabine

Stories about strong characters and characters who discover their strengths.

SERIES

Assassins Of The Dead- Young Adult Fantasy/ Paranormal

Book 1: Dark Blade

Book 2: Dragon Touched

Book 3: Society Against Vampires

Book 4: King's Request

Dragon Blood- Young Adult Urban Fantasy (with elements of romance)

(5 book series)

Book 1: Pliethin

Book 2: Wyvern

Book 3: Surety

Book 4: Knight

Book 5: Mage

Dragon Mage- Young Adult Urban Fantasy (with elements of romance)

(Series two of Dragon Blood series)

Book 1: Promise

Dragon Blood Chronicles- Young Adult Urban Fantasy (with elements of romance)

(Companion stand alone series to Dragon Blood)

Book 1: Oath

Book 2: Betrayed

Guardians Of The Round Table- Young Adult Fantasy LitRPG

(Co-written with Storm and Rhys Petersen)

Book 1: Dexterity Fail

Book 2: Goblin Boots

Book 3: Singed Feathers

Book 4: Frog Mage

Book 5: Crystal Mine

Book 6: Cursed Harp

Rosie's Rangers- Young Adult Western Steampunk

(6 book series)

Book 1: Justice

Book 2: Vengeance

Book 3: Treachery

Book 4: Accused

Book 5: Wanted

Book 6: Corruption

Mark Of Kings- Children's Fantasy

(Upper middle grade/preteen)

(4 book series)

Book 1: The Arena

Book 2: The Island

Book 3: The Assassin

Book 4: The King

STAND ALONE SERIES

Demon Hunters- Young Adult Urban Fantasy/ Horror (with elements of romance)

Book 1: Blood Sacrifice

Book 2: Retribution

Book 3: Tainted

Book 4: Premonition

Book 5: Cursed

Book 6: Feud

Book 7: Extrication

Plea Of The Damned- Young Adult Urban Fantasy/Paranormal

(6 book series)

Book 1: Forgive Me Lucy

Book 2: Forgive Me Aiden

Book 3: Forgive Me Jena

Book 4: Forgive Me Kobe

Book 5: Forgive Me Marti

Book 6: Forgive Me Dawson

***Realms Of The Fae- Young Adult Urban Fantasy
(with elements of romance)***

The Sword (short story)

Heart Of Stone

Book 1: A Debt Owed

Book 2: Marked By The Hunt

Book 3: The Magic Collector

Book 4: An Unexpected Betrayal

Book 5: Imprisoned By Iron

Fairytales Retold (Short Stories)

Snow-White And Rose-Red

The Twelve Brothers

The Light Princess

Beauty And The Beast

Sleeping Beauty

Aschenputtel

Myths And Legends Retold (Short Stories)

Ion, Son Of Apollo

Sir Gawain And The Maid With The Narrow Sleeves

Princess Ilse, The Giant's Daughter

YOUNG ADULT NOVELS

Young Adult Fantasy (with elements of romance)

Elf Sight

Earth Bound

Young Adult Urban Fantasy

Stone Warrior (with elements of romance)

The Jungle Inside

Young Adult Contemporary (with elements of romance)

Through Your Eyes

The Ugly Stepsister

Perfect Little Princess

Young Adult Contemporary/Paranormal

Whispers In The Dark (with elements of romance and same sex relationships)

Over Too Soon (with elements of romance)

Young Adult Sci-Fi

Experiment X-One-Six (Urban Sci-Fi/Superheroes)

An Endless Dawn (Post Apocalyptic Sci-Fi)

CHILDREN'S BOOKS

Dragon Lord (Preteen/early teens) (Fantasy)

The Irish Wizard (Upper middle grade) (Urban Fantasy)

SHORT STORIES

Urban Fantasy

Eternally Late

Dealings With Joe

Glimpses (short story in That Moment When Anthology)

Contemporary

The Brat Next Door

Fantasy LitRPG

(Set in the same world as Guardians Of The Round Table Series)

Tales Of Inadon 1: The Disc (Co-written with Storm and Rhys Petersen) (short story in Game On! Anthology)

Post Apocalyptic Sci-Fi

Compulsive Directive

NONFICTION

A Year Of Weekly Writing Exercises (Creative Writing)

Cooking For Families With Allergies (Cooking)
(Co-written with Storm Petersen)

Tell Me A Story, Grandma (Memoir)

For the most up to date details on available titles visit:

www.avrilsabine.com/books/bibliography

Realms Of The Fae Series

To learn more about this series visit:

www.avrilsabine.com/series/rotf

BOOKS AVAILABLE IN THE REALMS OF THE FAE SERIES

The Sword (short story in Like A Girl Anthology)

Heart Of Stone

Book 1: A Debt Owed

Book 2: Marked By The Hunt

Book 3: The Magic Collector

Book 4: An Unexpected Betrayal

Book 5: Imprisoned By Iron

Disclaimer

This is a work of fiction. Names, characters, businesses, places, events and incidents are either the products of the author's imagination or used in a fictitious manner. Any resemblance to actual persons, living or dead, or actual events is purely coincidental.